# Peppino and the Streets of Gold

*Titles available in this series:*

*Peppino, Good As Bread*
*Peppino and the Streets of Gold*

catree books

# Peppino and the Streets of Gold

by
Ann Rubino

Text copyright © 2016 Ann Rubino

Cover art copyright Julie Sulzen 2016

Library of Congress PCN: Pending

Peppino and the Streets of Gold/Ann Rubino [cover by Julie Sulzen] – 1st ed.

978-1-942247-07-4 (paperback)

978-1-942247-08-1 (hardcover)

978-1-942247-09-8 (digital)


1. Fiction_Historical  2. Children's Fiction

I. Rubino, Ann.

PRINT EDITION

10 9 8 7 6 5 4 3 2 1      Published by www. catree.com in Evanston, IL

# Dedication

For all the young people who search
for the gold and find it in themselves.

# Chapters

## Chapter I
# Beans, Beans, Beans

BANG! The bus lurched forward and jolted to a stop. Diving under the seat, I covered my head expecting another explosion. *"Maledetto demonio!"* (curse the devil) swore the bus driver. "The tire blew! It will cost a fortune at the black market—if I can even find one. You boys will have to walk the rest of the way. Get going, now. It's only another two kilometers. You can make it to the circus if you hurry."

*Madonna!* I thought we hit a land mine. I thought the Germans finally did it. They got us, a bunch of students riding home from Bari Middle School on the school bus. Shaken, I grabbed my book bag and scrambled off of the floor. I jumped out of the bus onto the broken road. The streets were so damaged from bombs and tanks that there was no way to avoid scuffing my new shoes. Stupid war! The Nazis and Fascists destroyed our homes and farms with their stupid war, but now that it's over, who shows up to rebuild our roads? Nobody. I could feel the dust seeping into my suit. Mamma would have a fit.

I ran up the front stairs to our home and stopped to dust my shoes with my sleeve. Boy, they looked awful. I even chipped the heel. As Mamma opened the door she shouted, "*Piano, piano* (slow down). Is the devil chasing you?" She took one look at my dirty suit and shook me by the arm. "Peppino! What have you done? Have you no respect for new clothes? Your father sent those shoes all the way from America. How could you ruin them so fast?"

"It wasn't my fault, Mamma," I protested as she dragged me into the house by my sleeve and started dusting me off, a little too hard. Nonna Paola, my mother's mother, was there too. She marched over to examine me as well.

"What's the matter with you? How do you tear your pants hem going to school? Are you crazy? Your mother sews all week to dress you like a proper young man and this is the thanks she gets?"

Before she could say any more I interrupted. "The bus, the tire blew." I retold the story, and both Mamma and Nonna calmed down somewhat.

Mamma said, "Well, those shoes have to last the whole year. Go downstairs and polish them. But change into your old clothes first. I don't want shoe polish on your school clothes."

I hurried into my room to change, all the while

hearing Nonna scold Mamma for being too soft on me. "How do you know the bus tire blew, Lucia? Eh? He's a boy, he's a liar, they all are. He makes it up. You're too soft. In my day a smack to the head and they don't lie any more." I quickly ran past them through the kitchen toward the cellar door. "Ay!" Nonna yelled and waved the back of her arm towards my head. I ducked and kept running down to the cellar to repair my shoes.

A few minutes later Nonna left and the quiet returned. "I'm hungry," I called up to Mamma. "What's there to eat?"

"Whatever you find in the garden," was her reply. The same old thing. The garden was behind our house inside a high stone wall with pieces of broken glass on top. Peppers, tomatoes, escarole, onions, garlic and an orange tree grew there. That's what we ate, but now in early fall, we had eaten most of it, and Mamma had made nearly all the tomatoes into sauce. The orange tree wouldn't blossom for a few months. I was really tired of escarole and endive, which still grew when it was cool. I picked an armful of dandelions brought them in and slammed them down on the counter in the kitchen. "Here Mamma." I grumbled. "Same as yesterday, and the day before that and the day before that."

"Shame on you! We have more important things to worry about. Your Uncle Carlo has been acting strange since he came back from the war— not sleeping, acting angry and smashing things, shouting at Nonna Paola. He really worries me, he's so changed." She took the dandelions and began to

clean them. "And I have no real help with the farms.
You're too little to be of much use, and Nonno's leg
holds him back. Don't complain to me."

This would be our dinner. Boiled dandelions.
Even with oil and beans and homemade cheese,
it was getting old. I was getting very sick of Italy.
We had nothing after the war and the stores were
empty. Things should be better by now but here I am
hungry, eating dandelions and beans. I never want to
see another bean.

Mamma handed me a watery cup of coffee
and some dry, hard bread. "It's the last piece, I saved
it for you." I kept quiet. "I went to the black market
today to get flour but they were out of it. We just have
to forget about sugar or coffee. They said they'd have
some flour tomorrow if another ship comes in. So
I'll have some bread for you tomorrow after school.
Don't worry. You'll see. Everything will be OK."

Yeah, everything would be OK. "But Mamma,
the war's over. So how come Italy isn't any better
than before? What was the fighting for anyway?"

"The Fascists are gone, life will return to
order. We live in the most beautiful house in the
town. Your father sends money. We live better than
most." It all fell on deaf ears. She always spoke of this
father of mine, living in America, where the streets
were paved with gold. Sure, he sent us some money.
We got a few packages from America. Sometimes
he sent clothes, sometimes American pasta. We
didn't eat that fancy pasta. It was made in a factory,
perfectly cut, each noodle the exact same size. We
saved it to give it to the teachers to get me good
grades. He also sent an envelope with American

money. Mamma stashed that immediately. She never told me where she hid it. This last time he sent shoes for me. The shoes were too small because he doesn't even know how big I have grown. "I don't think I have a real father," I shouted. "I think you made him up." Before she could swat me I ran into my bedroom and locked the door.

But I didn't stay there long. The circus was coming to town and we boys planned to watch the set up. I straightened my bed coverlet and ran out of my room. "Where are you going?" she shouted to me.

"The Circus!" I slammed the door behind me. She called something back, but her voice was muffled because I had already leapt off of the stairs and was running down the street. Closer to the piazza I slowed to a walk to catch my breath.

All morning during class as the teacher had droned on, I kept thinking about what a great life the circus people must have. They put everything they own in a wagon and go someplace else. They travel with the whole family together, too. "Keep your mind on your work, Binetti," the math teacher had commanded, slapping a ruler on my desk. "You've made three mistakes on the last paper—you used to be good at math. What's going on?"

"Sorry, *Signore Maestro,*" I told him, but the idea kept tumbling over in my mind... just pack up and go.

Getting off the bus after school, I saw that the parade from the morning was over and the men were starting to put up the tent. The *Campo Sportivo* was in bad shape after the Nazis had used it as a parking lot last year. Heavy trucks and tanks had worn away the grass and there were deep ruts where they had driven in the rain. Over to one side a big scorched spot and a pit showed where the ammunition dump had blown up. Nobody could play soccer there any more anyway so the circus chose that place to set up.

Dominic was already there. It was no surprise. He was always on top of the action. Mimmo, as always, tagged along. The raggedy wagon built on a small truck was parked on the *Campo Sportivo*. The lettering on its side read: *Circolo Equestre—Ludovico Il Magnifico & Famiglia."* (Circus—Louis the Great & Family). Under a temporary shelter a lady was tying back her bright yellow hair and changing into work clothes. Three small ponies with ragged, dirty ribbons tied to their manes were hitched to a post and a boy was piling hay for them. A couple of little kids sat on the dirt playing with three small dogs. We walked in to see what was going on.

Two men had started fencing in a big circular area with thin wooden panels. Another man carried boards and blocks, and set them up as benches inside the ring. They unpacked long poles, coils of rope, huge iron spikes as long as my arm, and a few heavy hammers. A big drum was propped along the side of the dressing tent. A boy was stringing a long electric cable across the field to plug it in at the nursery school across the road. We crossed the street to meet him.

"Binetti, Peppino," I said holding out my hand. "That looks heavy. Can I help?"

"Why do you want to help? We can't pay you.

You'll have to buy a ticket like everybody else." He dropped the cable to shake my hand. He was thin, about as tall as me with a tanned face and a mop of black hair. His arms were ropy with muscle and his work shirt was too big for him. He picked up the cable and continued to lay it out.

"I'll help you for free if I can talk to you about the circus—what it's like. I'm going to bring Mamma and Nonno, my grandfather, tonight."

"Trade talk for work—sounds good to me. I can talk a lot, too much my father says. He's Ludovico and he's not so '*magnifico*'. He's hard to work for; I might as well be a slave." He pointed to his father, the boss, with his chin.

"Get that power over here, Enzo, we have a show to set up!" Ludovico bellowed.

"*Si, Papá!*" he shouted.

"See, I told you... Let's get a move on." He put the end of the rope in my hand and pointed. "Here, take this end and walk toward my father. I'm Enzo. Get your friends to help, not just stand around."

I did as told. It was heavy work, even with Dom, Mimmo, and me all helping. The power cable was attached to a motor. The motor wound the cables to lift the tent. Ludovico hooked everything together. The other circus workers, Enzo, my friends and I each took hold of a rope to guide it straight. Slowly the tent rose, as high as a house, pointed in the middle. "If we attached the ropes in two places, it could go faster," Dom advised.

"When I need amateur advice, I'll ask for it,"

Ludovico retorted. He put the motor in neutral and handed each of us a spike and a hammer. "Put the spike on a slant through the loop in this rope. Put your energy into pounding, not talking. Pound it in well. Once they're in, we will pull up the tent the rest of the way."

He and the other man pounded in each stake with four strokes, while we kids tried not to hit ourselves by mistake. Enzo put his down in eight hits. Dom pounded hard because he was mad, but missed a lot and finally hit his toe. I missed a lot of times too but finally got the spike into the earth. Once they were all in, the motor started pulling up the tent toward the sky. As it rose I saw all the patches, even the new one the lady fixed while we were pounding.

As soon as that was done, they hooked up more ropes that pulled up a trapeze in the center. The yellow-haired lady walked over to the center and took hold of a rope that hung from the trapeze frame. She climbed it so fast it looked like she floated to the top. She practiced swinging back and forth, upside down getting closer and closer to the trapeze. My friends and I stood there gawking for about a minute until Ludovico saw us. "That's it, boys. You need a ticket for the rest. Nothing free in this world, you know. Thanks for the help." Ludovico waved toward the entrance and gave us a gentle push.

On the way out I asked Enzo, "Do you go everywhere? Do you have to go to school? Where do you sleep?"

"Here, carry this straw for the horse beds," he said, "We've got to keep busy. Follow me."

Dom, Mimmo and I hurried towards the camp stopping to dump the straw near the horses. Enzo pulled down a set of wooden steps at the back of a wagon. "This is my house. I sleep along the left side, on the blankets on those prop boxes. My dad and mother are along the front on the floor, and the kids have the straw padding on the other side. The dogs sleep in the middle. Our clothes hang on those hooks above, or in the costume chest. My books are in that box under the driver's seat. We cook outside on a wood fire and get our water from wells along the way."

Enzo climbed into the wagon and grabbed a fancy satin shirt. "This is the shirt I wear in the show. I have to practice while wearing this because the sleeves dangle and get in my way when juggling." He began to change.

"What about school?"

"My mother teaches me to read and count," he said. "She can read books if she has them. Not my father, though. He says he learns by living and watching. When he has to sign a contract he puts an X and mother writes his name next to it. I'm trying to learn different kinds of Italian so I can tell clown jokes. People in the north think *Napoletani* sound funny, and in Naples they laugh at the *Toscani*. I can tell the same joke in both places, just change the way I say the words. Everybody thinks the people around Bari talk funny, so I need to listen to more people before I go, to get the sounds right."

"Enzo!" His dad shouted, "we've got work to do. Send your friends off."

"I'm coming," he shouted to his dad. "Come

on," he said to me as we hustled to the exit. "We never have time off. Mamma and Silvia fix costumes and make new ones, and make clothes for the kids. You saw what the men do. We get a chance to wash and clean our clothes and look around the towns—maybe buy a few things if the take has been good. And then we're off to a new place. Rehearsal is every day, no matter what. If we miss our cue somebody might get hit with flying balls or fall off the trapeze. There's no net under my mother—did you notice? One slip and she's dead. So she practices all the time. The animals have to practice too. We always feed the horses, because they have to be strong and steady, but the dogs get fed when they perform. If they don't work, they don't eat."

"That's mean," I said. "What if they can't do it?"

"They do it, they have to. They're hungry. We don't ask them to do anything that's impossible—just work hard and obey."

We arrived at the exit.

"Maybe I can see your house too?" He asked.

"Of course," I replied. And we left. But I felt ashamed. His wagon would fit in our storage, where we lived during the war. How could I tell him about our inside bathroom and our running water in the kitchen? About Mamma's big bed that had room for two people to roll over, our fireplace and the clean cistern and our strong doors that kept out the wind? No, nobody has it good around here. The place is all torn up and destroyed. I probably have it the best and I'm still hungry. I raced home to tell Nonno.

*Chapter 2*
# Il Spettacolo (the show)

"Mamma, Mamma," I called, tracking mud all over the floor with my wet shoes. "*Sporcaccione*," (you dirty kid) she shouted, grabbing a rag to wipe my tracks.

I untied my shoes and put them at the door. "The Circus is almost set up. They brought everything in little wagons. It's a family business." I rattled off all that I had seen, finishing with, "we never had a circus before."

"They had dogs inside? They must be dirty people, *disgraziati*!"

"Maybe—but I want to see what they do. Can we go tonight, Mamma? Please, please, please?"

"You have to take care of our animals and do your homework first. The circus won't get you a job later."

"I can pay for it, Mamma. I saved up some *lire* (money) from selling cigarettes."

"What cigarettes? What saving? Why didn't you tell me?"

"Only a hundred *lire*, Mamma, like you told me. Work and save. I can take you as my guest. You and Nonno."

She stared at me for a minute, undecided.

"I did tell you to work hard," she said finally. "I'll take your offer. We'll go—you pay. Now about those chores."

"Yes, Mamma." I did my chores as fast as I could. I went outside and pushed the hens off their nests to get the eggs. I fed and watered the goat and cleaned her pen. I fed the rabbits and cleaned them too. Then I gathered an armload of firewood from the tall pile and brought it in for the stove.

Nonno came by just then, letting himself in through the iron gate. He always came over to see me after school. "Nonno, Nonno!" I squealed, running back through the garden.

"*Calma, calma,*" (calm down) Nonno said, as he placed his big, gentle hands around my shoulders and kissed each cheek. "How is my Peppino today?"

"Very good Nonno. The circus came, I went inside!"

"Oh, so that is the excitement. I saw them go by my house to set up."

"Nonno, I have enough to buy three tickets. I want you to be my guest."

"Oh my. How can you afford tickets?"

So I told Nonno all about the cigarettes and

how I saved them and sold them to make money.

"You are a very industrious boy, just like your father."

"What's my father like, Nonno? I wish I knew him. He was your boy. Don't you miss him?"

"He is a very hard working man. He is a good man. You know he sends things to you and your mamma even from the other side of the world."

"But I want to see him, I want to go to America."

Nonno paused and looked out through the iron garden gate. A donkey cart with hay was passing on the dusty street. "It's true, Peppino. This isn't much of a life here in Italy. It's true that we have always been hungry. We have always struggled to get along. Your father went to America when he was 16 looking for work. And he found it, because he works very hard. I've been sad having him far away. I worry about him, but he is with his cousins anyway. And I still have my other son here, and my daughters.

"Peppino, you have to understand, your father is not away from you by choice. It is because in America there are jobs and farms and money. The country is so much better than here. Everything is new. Everything works. It is such a rich country people say the streets are paved with gold."

"Really Nonno? Real gold?"

"It's a saying my boy. It means that it is the richest country in the world. No matter where you come from, no matter how poor you are, in America if you work hard you can make a good life. This is why my boy went, to get a job and send money home."

"That's why I want to go too Nonno!" I cried.

"Yes, I know. I can't say I blame you. You're young, you deserve to be able to make a better life."

"But Mamma won't want to go."

"Well your mother has her life here, her family, her ways. But I think maybe someday, if your father stays there with a good job, your mother might agree to go."

"But I would miss you the most, Nonno," I said.

"Yes, and I would miss you too. But what kind of father would hold his children back? I would not make you stay your whole life here just for me, any more than I'd make your father stay here. I understand a man needs to have his dreams. A man needs to find his own place. I would miss you if you left, Peppino. But I would hold you in my heart just the same." That was all Nonno had to say.

By now I was sure, I would go to America. I only had to figure out a way.

Mamma and Nonno enjoyed the circus. Ludovico juggled all kinds of things—small colored balls, big fluffy balls, empty wine bottles. He and his wife juggled together, throwing things back and forth. Enzo, with a white face and clown suit, juggled with Ludovico and only dropped one bottle. The other lady made the dogs dance and jump through a hoop. She rode on the horse, too, and stood up on one foot waving flags. Her husband balanced a long pole on his head while their two young daughters climbed up it and waved. What a family!

"They're hard workers," Mamma said as we walked home. "That's what a family is for—working together. But I'd rather grow our food and not depend on people putting down *lire* for a ticket. Did you see how thin those little girls are?"

"Maybe they have to be skinny to climb up on that pole," I said.

"Or maybe there isn't much to eat. All of them are skinny. Dirty too."

"That's true. But we are hungry too, and at least they have each other, while our family is all torn apart. Mamma, I want to go to America! I want to live with Papá! Why can't we go to America?" Mamma shot a glance at Nonno who was walking with his eyes down to the road.

"What is this again, Peppino? What is this desire to go to America? You keep bothering me about it. We live here."

"Mamma, Papá is there. We can't be a family if one of us is missing."

"Peppino, we have discussed this already, many times. Our life is here, our family, our farms, our house, your grandfather--"

Nonno interrupted, "Don't look at me, Lucia. I didn't hold my sons back and I won't hold my grandson back either."

Mamma pursed her lips. "So, I see. Well anyway, our life is here."

I wouldn't give it up. "Mamma, your life may be here, but I am young. I have more life ahead of me than you."

"For shame," Mamma scolded. "Are you

wishing me to die, after all I've done for you?"

"The boy is right, you know," Nonno challenged. "A man has to go forward, build up his future."

I kept arguing, "There is no future here. You saw it. Look at those circus people. They are hungry. Our whole town is hungry and it's not getting better."

"Well, we'll have to see," she replied. And that was the end of that. I looked over at Nonno. He winked at me and smiled, but we walked home in silence.

*Chapter 3*

# Suspicion

I spied Angelina *ficcanaso,* my mother's gossipy friend, in the piazza near the fountain. Angelina reminded me of *La Befana,* the good witch who brings gifts to kids at Epiphany. But she didn't bring gifts. She brought news. She knew everything that went on in town and spread the news around like seeds in a field, even if she had to make some of it up. She leaned on her cane, even more bent over than usual. Her black dress was threadbare and she had holes in her slippers. With her long black shawl wrapped over her straggly gray hair and her bent back she didn't seem very lively, but her black eyes glittered with craftiness. She looked cold. I was cold too. It was getting chilly and the fall damp pierced through my father's old thread-bare jacket. I shivered a little as I walked up to her. I'd better get more

firewood when I get home or the beds will feel like
ice tonight. I caught up with her. She was heading
toward my house. *"Ciao, Commar' Angelina.* How
are you feeling?"

"Not so good, but I'm still living. Are you
going home now? I'll walk with you. I haven't seen
your mother for a while." We made our way down the
street, stepping around the bigger puddles. It looked
like it might rain again, and it felt good once we were
inside. I could smell the sweet smoke from the olive
wood sticks in the *braciere* (fire pan) and walked
over to toast my hands over the fire.

*"Commar' Angelina's* here, Mamma," I
shouted. Mamma came out of the kitchen wiping her
hands on a towel. "How nice to see you, *Commar',"*
touching her face to Angelina's cheek. "Come in and
rest a little. What brings you out on a rainy day?"

"Just a visit, my dear. Just a chat. I see you
have baked cookies." She settled herself in the
wooden rocking chair in the kitchen and let her shawl
drop over the back. "What do you hear from your
Gino in America?"

"He writes all the time," Mamma said, looking
sideways at me. "The goat needs food and water,
Peppino. And we need eggs for supper. Out you go,
now."

"Can't I just have a cookie?"

"One— and then do your chores. Angelina will
keep me company."

I knew when I wasn't wanted, so I went
through the door to go downstairs where the
animals lived, and closed it behind me. I heard their

voices begin as I stood on the top step holding my breath. "Grazia DiNardi has a heavy cross to bear," Angelina said.

"Whatever do you mean," Mamma asked. "Does she have cancer?"

"No, worse." Angelina said in a low voice. "Betrayal. Men are not to be trusted. My cousin in Chicago wrote that Grazia's husband has a lady friend, an American. She smokes and wears makeup. And the packages have stopped coming."

"No packages? How can she get along?"

"She's selling some of her furniture and plans to go to America. She's going to take her family back."

"Oh, the poor thing. *Poverella!*" Mamma said.

Angelina stirred her coffee and picked up another cookie. "What do you hear from Gino?"

"Oh, he's doing well. He's the leading cook at the candy factory. He sends packages all the time—pasta, the coffee you're drinking, even American money."

"I'm happy to hear that. So many men's eyes wander when they're far from home. You'd be shocked at what I hear. At least six women from this town have left for America since summer. All because of their wandering husbands."

Crouching on the top step, I couldn't believe my ears. We haven't had any packages for two months, and no money either. What was Mamma talking about? The voices went on for a while. Mamma sounded like she was selling Papá to Angelina. Angelina sounded like she wasn't sure she wanted to buy. I heard the chair scrape back and then footsteps, so I scrambled downstairs to feed the goat. When I heard the front door close I went back upstairs. The goat could wait. "Did we get the package?" I wanted to know. "Did Papá send a letter?"

"No. *Niente*. Not a thing." A tear rolled down Mamma's cheek. "Now it's more than two months." She rubbed her eyes with her apron and shook her head. "He won't get away with it," she announced. "We're going there. No American is going to take my Gino."

The next day I went to school as usual, and got hit on my hand for messing up my pages, so I was in a sour mood as I walked in the door. You should have seen the house! Mamma was packing up stuff like she was a tornado. She had our clothes laid out on the bed and she was sorting: keep, give away, sell, keep, give away, sell. "We're going to America. First you will have First Communion and we get the passports. We can be ready by Christmas. Here, help me sort these things." What was she saying? Going to America? But she was crying at the same time. Her face was red and I didn't know if she was going to blow up or what. Slam went a dress; a pair of shoes hit the floor with a crash.

"What's going on, Mamma?" I shouted. "You're going crazy here."

"It's your Papá," she almost spit out his name. "Angelina thinks he may have a *commara*—a girl friend, in America. Angelina says she is suspicious. After I prayed for him every night with a candle under his picture! That girl will wish she never met him. We're going there and I'm taking back my family. You won't be 12 until after Christmas so you can go for half fare. Thursday we'll go to Naples to get our passports and tickets—a visa for me, too. Aunt Graziella will take care of our furniture, Nonno will watch the house and the animals, Dominic's father will run the farms. No American with makeup is going to break up our family!"

I didn't know whether to laugh or cry. I wanted America, but not like this. What was the matter with Angelina, hurting Mamma with her gossip? Mamma never did anything to her. When Papá wrote last spring and said he missed us and wanted me to talk Mamma into going to America, it seemed like a good idea.

*Chapter 4*
# Making Our Move

Next morning we were at the train station by dawn. The train for Naples was exactly on time. Mussolini was good for that at least. People lined up for permission to leave Italy. We bribed a couple of clerks in the passport office to get our passports fast. It took a couple of trips to the American Embassy to get Mamma's visa, but my birth certificate proved that I was born after my father became an American citizen. I was officially an American. I never knew that! So I got an American passport that allowed me to officially bring my mamma to America with me. Imagine—I was taking Mamma and not the other way around.

At the ticket office she reached down deep into the front of her dress and brought up a roll of dollars that she had been saving all along. She bought two tickets to sail from Naples to New York right after Christmas. We would cross the Atlantic that I'd only seen on the school map, in the middle of winter. Cold or not, rough waves or not, ready or not, we were going. What I had always wished for was going to happen, and all because of a rumor.

Mamma was really ready to go this time, but it wasn't so simple to shift our lives to America. The first obstacle we met was her mother, Nonna Paola. We went to tell her our news and she was like another volcano. "How can you desert me in my old age?" she cried. "After all I've done for you? I carried you for nine months. I nursed you and fed you when you were a baby..." Nonna Paola was getting old, but her memory was strong. She remembered every mistake Mamma had ever made, and every dress or meal Nonna had ever given her. Mamma always ended up sad after these visits and she wouldn't talk much for a day or two.

"I have a husband too, Mother. I should be at his side—like we said in church. Remember?"

"Words, words! What are they compared to a mother's sacrifices? A mother gives her whole life to her children, especially daughters. And this is what she gets—a slap in the face. Ingratitude! Betrayal! A mother can raise 12 children, but those 12 children cannot help their mother." Nonna's words stung Mamma like a whip.

"Please, Mother—my marriage vows before God are important. My husband needs me. I can come back and visit."

I wandered out of the room and let

them struggle. I watched *Zia* Nina running the hemstitching machine. "Kerplunk, kerplunk, kerplunk" it went, slowly sewing neat tiny holes around the hem of a tablecloth. "Do you think she'll let us go, *Zia*?" I asked.

"She can't really stop you, but she can take all the joy out of it," she replied dryly. "She's good at that. Every time we start to have any fun around here—a little laughing, maybe a visitor—she manages to make us miserable."

"Maybe she doesn't know any better," I said. "Maybe she thinks that's the way it ought to be."

"*Forse* (maybe)—but it's hard on me and your uncle. She thinks smiling is a sin. Nothing we do is good enough. Carlo wakes up screaming every night and gets angry about nothing. He wanders around in the piazza and seems confused. I think something happened to his mind in the war. It isn't our fault that our father died, or the boys sailed away or the war happened! Nothing pleases our mother, no matter how hard we try. It isn't easy for any of us."

I went back to see who was winning, and Mamma almost ran me over. She was heading for home, Nonna's voice shouting behind her. "You've betrayed your mother! You'll never have any good luck in your life now. Your life will be cursed."

Mamma grabbed me by the elbow with tears in her eyes and an angry set to her mouth. As we walked, a couple of people started to say *Ciao*, then ducked their heads and stepped back. Mamma in a bad mood was a force of nature. "No wonder my brothers left young for America," she sputtered. "They were smarter than I thought. Too bad if my mother's sad. She's mad at everybody and drives them away. May her curse bounce back on her!"

Nonno Giuseppe, Papá's father, was cut from kinder cloth. He was gentle and mellow—faithful as an old horse. "I'll take care of your property and the garden. That's what I'm good for, after all. If I sell anything, I'll send you the money. Your property is safe and you'll find it when you return. Only the goat. I want to sell her. It's getting hard for me to do the milking every morning. My old leg injury from the Great War bothers me a lot and I have to use the cane all the time."

Mamma smiled the first smile I'd seen in three days. "I am so glad I can depend on you! You have taken care of me like your own daughter during all the war. Gino takes after you. It will be so good to see him after all these years! And I don't care what you do with the goat."

"Will you come to see us?" I asked Nonno. "Who's going to help us in America?"

"It's too far, Peppino. You'll be with your Papá. He'll take care of you both."

"Maybe I can come back to see you," I said.

"Maybe. Maybe a miracle. No, you'll be happy in America. Don't worry about me. I still have children here to fill my heart. Nonna Claudia and my girls are a lot of company."

We passed the word to our close friends to see if anyone wanted to rent the house. So many homes were damaged that plenty of renters could be found, but Mamma loved her house. She didn't want it in careless hands. As soon as my uncle the surveyor heard about it he rushed over right away. "We'll take it," he said. "Name your price."

"But Antonio, there's no office downstairs for your business. It's a house for a farmer. You don't have any use for the storage. Why pay for it?"

"I can make my office there, change the big *portone* for a smaller door. The bomb broke the back wall of my house, remember? It's only patched with wood. I can get that repaired and rent it out to people from the city. I'll make enough to pay your rent, and we'll have running water and plumbing. Nina will be so happy with that, and a garden besides. Please say yes. We'll keep it safe for when you come back."

"You have it then. Promise when we come back you'll give it up?"

"I promise."

We still needed somebody to take care of the farms, as we called them, narrow fields of almonds, grapes and olives. Somebody had to look after the grapes, getting them pruned and harvested on time. Somebody had to prune the olives and the almonds and oversee those harvests too. Rocks working their way to the surface needed to be built into the walls around the land. Land couldn't just take care of itself. "How about Dominic's father?" I asked her. "Or is he too mean?"

"He's strong, all right, and he won't steal from us. If he's mean he'll guard our fields. Maybe we can pay Dominic to help him. It would help their family too." He agreed to run the farm, take his share for pay and send us the rest. Mamma insisted that Dominic get paid too so he didn't have to steal.

"I'm coming to America as soon as I save up," Dominic whispered in my ear. "Whether they want me to or not. Once I'm fifteen I can go anyplace. Watch for me! One day I'll just appear!" Mamma got my uncle the surveyor to write up a contract and she and Dominic's father signed it. There were three copies—one for us, one for Dominic's father and one for my uncle to keep in his file at the office. Mamma didn't take any chances!

**Chapter 5**

# Final Preparations

I thought packing would be easy. The circus people could pack in half a day and move on. But I found out it wasn't so simple. "You need better clothes," she told me. "Your pants are too short and your jacket sleeves are worn."

"Papá won't care," I replied. "They have clothes in America."

"Nonsense. The cloth on your father's old suits is still strong. I can make a suit in a few days. What will he think if I bring him his son in rags? It would be shameful." She took the suits apart into a thousand pieces, cut all the pieces smaller, and then sewed them into a suit again. She did the same with four shirts. She even made me new underwear.

I traded almonds with some sailors for socks. Mamma made herself three dresses and took her old coat apart and rearranged the cloth pieces so it looked new. She found an old fur jacket that was worn out and took a piece from the best part to make a collar. She wanted to "make *una bella figura*" when she arrived in New York.

Then there was the mattress problem—how to pack it, how to carry it. I wondered why to take it at all. Don't they have beds in America? They must have mattresses too. Probably Papá has been sleeping on a mattress all these years, if America was so nice. I said that to Mamma.

"My mother saved her *lire* and bought all the wool to make that mattress for my wedding. She washed it and stuffed it to fill up the cover. They don't do that in America! All their things are from factories, from strangers, made by machines. We're not leaving that behind."

"Mamma, I think Papá must already have one," I said cautiously. "It's really heavy and big. Where will we put it on the ship?"

"Ships can carry airplanes. They can carry bombs and trucks. They can carry my mattress." I couldn't change her mind.

Then the bad news struck in Papá's letter. "The bed frames in America will only hold a mattress 137 cm wide," he wrote. Mamma's treasured mattress was more than a foot wider. It would have to be taken apart and re-made to fit. This all happened before Christmas and we were leaving right after. The tickets had already been paid for. Mamma located a mattress maker in Bari and we paid a man with a car to take it and us into town. Mamma sat in front while

I and the mattress were jammed into the narrow
back seat. "I have to have it in one week," Mamma
told the craftsman after we hauled it into the shop.
"It's an emergency."

"Do you have someone coming home from the
hospital?" he asked.

"No, we're moving away and I must take it
with me." He gave her a puzzled look.

"Far away then? To a foreign land where there
are no beds? Libya maybe?"

"Don't concern yourself with my problems."
She lifted her chin and gave him a dirty look. "Can
I have it before Christmas? You notice I'm not
bargaining price. I'll pay you to hurry."

"All right, *Signora*. I'll do it. I'll have your
mattress ready. I'll put the extra wool in a sack too,
in case you want to use it for pillows. You may need
them when you get to the desert. And I'll deliver it by
Christmas Eve." She scowled at him as we went out.
"Desert indeed," she grumbled.

On the way home in the car, as we got close
to the *camposanto*, the cemetery, "*O Dio mio!* We
have to stop and say goodbye to all our departed!"
Mamma smacked herself on the forehead. "Let us out
here, please! We can walk the rest of the way," she
told the driver. She paid him and we went through
the big iron gates and walked down the stone path
between the *arborvitae* trees. Every cemetery had
them, in neat rows between the tombs and along the
edges inside the walls. You can spot a cemetery a
mile away. The stone and marble tombs were built in
long rows, like miniature apartments stacked up in

four or five layers. On the wall at the foot of each one was a bronze vase for the flowers the families would bring every week, the name of the person carved in the stone, and a picture in a small glass frame firmly attached to the stone. She brought me to see the grave of her father, my other grandpa, and we put a few bay branches and a couple of dried flowers into his vase. A flower stand stood outside the gate all year round so people could buy them there. Even during the worst of the war, people found a way to put flowers in the cemetery vases. "Here are my own grandparents," she said. " See, my sister is named after my grandma, as it should be."

I saw a baby picture and my own name carved under it! "That's me, Mamma," I exclaimed. "Is that ready for when I die?"

"That's your older brother, the first Peppino, who died when he was a baby. You carry his name, to keep it in the family." I never knew I had a brother. He must have died even before I was born.

I had to ask, "What happened to him, Mamma?"

"He got a bad cough and never got better. There was no medicine." She blinked a few times, then sniffed and straightened her shoulders. "I loved him, but now I have you and you are strong. I'm thankful for that at least." That explained a lot—all the sewing and feeding me liver and making me wear sweaters. As we went down the row she pointed out the other relatives, people I had never seen, but with familiar names. Looking at the long row of tombs was like a family tree, and you could find your grandparents, and their grandparents back for generations. "Never forget them," Mamma said. "Never forget where you come from." I promised.

"We still have to pack up my sewing machine," Mamma said the next morning. "I can't leave that behind either. We can do it while we're waiting for the mattress."

It was the same old conversation, just changing a few words: I'd say, "They have them in America." Then she'd say, "My mother saved up to give it to me." I was glad she wasn't so in love with her heavy dishes. I didn't mind packing the pots and pans. I remembered hiding those in the wall during the war.

I helped her take out the needles and take off the drive belt. We wired the treadle to keep it from moving. Paper labels with Papá's address in America went inside the cabinet, inside the bobbin drawer, and inside the chassis next to the gears—any place we could stick a piece of paper. Then we covered it tightly with burlap and wrapped ropes around it. We glued a big label on the outside of the burlap bundle, with an arrow showing the right side up. With its cast iron frame and wooden cabinet, I could only lift one end, but Mamma was sure we could carry it on the ship. "They could carry bombs," she said, "carry trucks..."

"I know, Mamma, they can carry a sewing machine too." She nodded in agreement.

Before Christmas we went to see Don Silvestro, our priest. "We need Peppino to have First Communion before Christmas," she told him. "I can't be taking him across the ocean until he's a full Christian."

"But the class is all planned for next May," Don Silvestro protested. "We never do it in Advent. Advent is a time of..."

"I know, I know, time to prepare. Well, we're preparing to leave Italy and go to America. Our preparing is more than putting purple decorations in church and making cookies. Our life is changing and we need you to help us. You know he's a good boy and he's studies his catechism. Just ask him something."

Don Silvestro looked down at me and said very seriously, "What is the most important commandment?"

"Love God first and your neighbor as your self," I recited.

"Do you do that?" he said. I had to think a while. "Dominic and I sort of lied to get flour tickets. We gave them away, though."

"You didn't steal them?"

"No."

"Well that's not a big sin. You helped somebody."

"I talked back to the *Hauptmann* when he was trying to catch Rachel, to send her away on a train to die—said I didn't know where she was."

"Did you know exactly how far she was from your house?"

"No, she was walking toward the farm."

"Well, then, you couldn't know just where she was, could you? And you protected her life. I'd say you know the commandments well enough." He turned to Mamma. "Next Sunday dress him up and bring him to church. He can march up to the altar with you." He smiled at Mamma. "And don't forget that I'm especially fond of those *pasta reale* cookies you make. Until next Sunday, then." He patted me on the shoulder and gestured toward the door. *"Ciao, Signora, e buon viaggio."* (Have a good trip).

So next Sunday after Mass all the cousins, aunts and uncles gathered at Nonna Claudia's house for my party. There were all kinds of cookies for dessert and Nonno gave me a silver American dollar that he had been saving since before the war in case of emergency. Don Silvestro came and ate seven almond cookies and two *biscotti*. Step by step we were moving toward America. The day before Christmas the mattress man drove up in an old car belching smoke. He had bundled the mattress up with ropes and put the leftover wool in a bag. He helped us haul it into the house and pile it up with the other items that were going with us on the ship. We were ready to go now, with only the good-byes tomorrow and then off to Naples to board the ship.

The next morning after Christmas Mass we went from one friend to another to say good-bye. All of our foreign friends had already shipped out to their home countries, and Rachel, our refugee friend, had gone back to the Rome ghetto to help her fiancé, Primo. We worked our way down one street and around to another, and there were lots of hugs and good wishes and tears. Nonna Claudia gave me a bag of her almond cookies to take on the train too, and a stick of *torrone* candy. "Stay sweet, Peppino," she said. "You are your parents' pride—don't disappoint them. Remember us always!" She wiped a tear away and smiled at me. "If I don't see you again—remember me."

"He'll come back one day, Claudia," Nonno said, patting her back to cheer her up. "He won't be able to stay away from your cookies." We stopped off at Nonna Paola's. Zia Nina hugged us and wished us good luck. Uncle Carlo stood silent with a sour look. When he shook my hand he said *"Ci vedemo"* (Be seeing you), which I thought was strange at the time.

Nonna Paola was very gloomy, knowing it was too late to stop us. "Be careful in America. If you see your brothers, remind them that they have a mother who thinks of them. Be a good wife. May you have better fortune than you deserve." She gave a quick hug and turned away. That was it. No turning back. We were off.

### Chapter 6
# On Our Way

We took the train the next day toward Naples, with our luggage, mattress and sewing machine packed in the baggage car. Several people from town were going on the same ship: two young men joining their fathers, a lady we didn't know who had moved in from Capurso before the war, and *Signora* DiNardi with Mimmo and his two younger sisters. Mimmo's mom was going to straighten out his father, whatever that meant, and she was bringing all her kids to help her straighten him. She sat next to Mamma on the hard leather seat the whole way, chattering about how things would be in America."You'll have to learn to talk American, Lucia. Get your hair fixed at the *parucchiere*. Put on lipstick."

"I won't feel like myself that way, Grazia! All false! My husband didn't marry me for that; he married be out of respect. He knew he could trust me with his home and property—that I wouldn't waste it on *stupitaggi*, nonsense. He's depended on me all this time. What will he think if I show up after all these years looking like a cheap stage actress?"

"He'll love it, Lucia! Men are silly that way. They live by their eyes. Don't you ever see how they watch all the girls passing by? They notice, all right. Even an honest man likes to have a pretty wife."

"Well, maybe I can get a haircut on the ship. I don't want to waste money on myself with a son to educate...It would all be *moneta spregata al vento* (money thrown to the wind)!"

"He doesn't need every penny! You are worth a lot yourself. You can get a job sewing at the suit factory and that money will pay for his education. There's more than one way to do business, Lucia! All my friends there do it. Money spent to keep your husband is a good investment."

Mimmo and I sat behind them, our feet propped up on our suitcases, watching the world fly by through the window. The wheels rattled clickety-click as the train rocked along. "Mimmo," I whispered. "Do the American wives sew in a factory? Don't they use their own sewing machines at home? We're bringing it with us so she can use it." I hated to waste all that work—packing and hauling the cumbersome thing.

"I don't know—maybe—but my mother heard the machines at the factory are really fast. They say a whole room full of women make suits all at once, with a hundred machines!"

"What a crazy place," I told him. "Mothers at a factory, fathers getting paid to make candy, people talking all different ways, telephones in every building...it's going to take getting used to. Do you think we'll like it?"

"We'd better get used to it," Mimmo said. "The grownups are running things. They probably know what they're doing."

For the rest of the train ride Mimmo and I played *scopa* on the seat between us, practicing to play with the big guys on the ship.

At the train station, we loaded ourselves into taxis and went to a hotel. It had six floors, and was taller than anything in our town, almost as tall as the church in Bari. It all looked new and much too fancy to live in. The lobby had marble floors and soft couches everywhere. Every room had a beautiful tile bathroom with towels that matched. The shiny bronze elevator doors looked like gold. An operator ran it up and down to all the floors, calling out the numbers as he stopped at each floor with a sickening lurch. Mimmo and I rode up and down until he finally told us. "If you can't make up your mind, get off and walk." He put us off on the top floor. We walked down the stairs to the 4th floor and found our families.

Supper was late that evening in the restaurant downstairs—all of us together. It was a "goodbye to Italy" party. Being in Naples, we had to start with pizza for appetizer, then *calamari* and soup. The pasta was good—sweeter than Mamma's and she complained that it was *troppo dolce*. There was not a single bean! We ate it all, along with the meat and the fruit and the *cannoli*. Those were the best! The *Napoletani* really know how to make pastries even if they do talk funny. After all that I was ready to sleep in a big bed with a mattress made by strangers. What a life—and just the first day!

*Chapter 7*
# On the Sea

I expected the ship to be big but it was tremendous. It was taller than any house I'd ever seen, and that was only the part sticking up out of the water. The taxi driver drove up pretty close to the gangplank and a couple of burly men came over with a cart to pile up our baggage. They struggled with the sewing machine and the woolen mattress, but Mamma wouldn't leave those behind. The pots and pans were in the trunk so they didn't get to comment on those, but they joked about the mattress. "Don't they have beds in America, *Signora*? I'm sure everyone there uses a bed, probably even the dogs."

"You can keep your thoughts to yourselves," she snapped. "This is my property and it's going with me." We marched up the gangplank after them, carrying our own personal suitcases.

At the top of the ramp, a clerk checked our tickets and documents, then pointed us towards the sleeping areas—down three flights of narrow metal ladder-like stairs and then down a corridor.

Halfway along the corridor, another clerk sorted us according to our tickets. There were big rooms full of bunk beds assigned by number. Some rooms were for women and girls and little kids, others for men. Mamma and her friends went with the women. All three were going together to join their husbands. They sent us boys to the men's area. My bed was number 3A in room 312. Mimmo got a bunk at the far end, 12B. Double-level bunks were lined up all along both sides of the long room. The ones on the bottom were marked A; the top ones reached by rickety ladders were marked B. Two other men from our town were there too, going to join their relatives who were already American citizens. Everyone was milling around, stowing suitcases under the beds, checking out the washing sinks at the end, looking for the bathroom and showers. The showers turned out to be public. They were big, cold, metal rooms, painted gray with plenty of shower spouts and no curtains for privacy.

"Why does this kid have a lower bunk? You mean I have to climb up all the time? What kind of a deal is this anyway? I paid full fare." I heard shouting and went back to see. A young guy in a brown checked suit was yelling at the steward, standing right by 3A. His dialect was hard to understand—maybe from Naples, maybe Sicily—I couldn't tell. He was about ½ a meter taller than me and looked

tough. He had a mustache and needed a haircut.
There was a scar on his cheek. He wore a silk tie, but
his shirt was spotted and dirty and needed fixing
around the collar. I didn't want to start out with
trouble.

"I can take the top bunk," I volunteered. "I'm a
good climber. It isn't a problem."

"OK, kid. A wise decision," he sneered. So now
I was 3B but in a safer spot. I was glad to see a couple
of men from our town in the same room. I'd have a
person to help me if things got ugly. There wasn't
much room to run in the ship, and Dominic was far
away at home. Mimmo couldn't lick a lemon, so he'd
be no help in a tight spot.

Once we were settled, most of the passengers
went up on the deck to watch us leave. As the
tugboats turned the ship around and guided it out
of the harbor I was thinking: No more Italy! Ten
days across the water and then America! Sailing is
easy—just sleep downstairs, walk around up here and
watch the water, don't have to feed any animals or go
to school, all kinds of fancy food. This is the life!

It took us about two days to get through
the Mediterranean, passing Sardinia and Corsica
toward Gibraltar. We stopped there to load more
passengers. The ship rocked so much we held on to
the handles that were everywhere along the walls,
but it was a pretty nice trip. Up on deck you could
watch the birds and see the big waves the ship made
as it sliced through the water. The big diesel engines
rumbled as we pushed along, making foamy waves
like mountains with white tops. Sometimes I could

see dolphins swimming alongside, and after meals, seagulls and other birds gathered at the back to grab the food scraps as the cooks threw them overboard.

In a large room upstairs, there was a big game board for chess on the floor where people could play by moving giant pieces. Everybody walked around the deck and people dressed up. A couple of people had cameras to take pictures of their lady friends. They didn't want me in their pictures, though—I asked and got many dirty looks. Another thing I found out was that we were staying in the tourist section where it was cheapest.

On the higher decks there were fancy rooms like a hotel with private sleeping rooms, a beautiful restaurant and even a ballroom with a stage for a band. There was a swimming pool and a library. I went up there alone one day to look around and they sent me back to the main deck. "This for the *prima classe*," they said. "You don't belong here. Go below with the other *contadini* (peasants)." I started to explain that I was a student going to America, not one of the *contadini* but the steward reached out to slap me so I ducked and ran back down. What an arrogant bunch of snobs, I thought. They think they're special because they have money. Some day I'll show them!

I spotted mountains rising out of the water at the end of the second day. There can't be mountains in the ocean. I asked a sailor and he laughed. "Those are the Pillars of Hercules," he said. "The end of the Mediterranean sea at Gibraltar. Once we go through the straits, the passage there, we'll get out into the real ocean. You'll see a change in the water color. The engines will really start working when the current starts to pull us. The wind may pick up a bit too."

Start working? I thought. Wind picking up? The engines have been roaring and grinding all night ever since we started. I can hear them rumble all the time in the sleeping room. The whole ship trembles like a scared rabbit when I sleep. And the wind is already slicing me into pieces. He knew what he was talking about, though. After our brief stop to take on new passengers, we went through the narrow straits with the mountain on our right, and the water got a lot rougher. The waves came up along the sides of the boat and we made sure to stay within reach of the railings. The deck chairs crashed into the railings as they slid back and forth. The wind blew colder, from the West. I wore both of my jackets and pulled my cap down around my ears. I kept blowing on my blue fingers to warm them. Maybe winter wasn't the best time to sail on the ocean.

After that people started to get sick. We had buckets in our sleeping room but often the people throwing up didn't get to them fast enough. Boy did it stink! The smell was so awful it made more people sick. All day long we went up and down and sideways, never knowing which direction we'd pitch next. Looking out the round windows I could see under the water sometimes, and then we'd go up and I'd see the foamy white tops of waves. There weren't many people coming to supper any more. Rims around the edges of tables kept the dishes from sliding off, and our dishes would slide here and

there, slopping spaghetti sauce and gravy across the
wooden tables.

Our dining room didn't have tablecloths like
the one upstairs so the waiters just wiped them with
big drippy gray cloths. The first rough night only
six came for supper—two ladies from Abruzzi, a guy
from my room, one big girl from Naples, Mamma
and me. Mimmo and his family were all in their
bunks, clinging to the sides with a bucket close just
in case. The supper was meat, a potato, and a strange
dessert. It was red and clear like glass, but soft and
wiggly. It tasted sweet like an odd fruit, and every
time the ship shifted, it trembled. Mamma took a
taste. "What is this wonderful stuff?" she exclaimed.

"It's called Jell-O," said the waiter. "It's
American food. They eat it all the time."

"How do they make it? Do you cook it?" She
was full of questions for the waiter, and he had plenty
of time on his hands as he stood there with a firm
grip on the table, rocking back and forth.

"You get a special powder and put boiling
water in it. Then you keep it cold all afternoon. It gets
sort of solid like this and you can make shapes with
it. They often mix in other things too, like shreds of
carrots or pieces of fruit." He seemed to be pretty
interested in Jell-O, or maybe in Mamma, because he
kept on explaining.

"I'm going to get that powder when we're
in America! What a good idea," Mamma told me
afterwards. "I could make it when it's too hot in the
house to cook." I wasn't crazy about it myself. It was
too wiggly and strange. Cookies are more reliable.

Your teeth have something to grab on to. Fruits were good too, and there was a store in the ship that sold big, green pears for 5 cents. They were American pears—bigger than my fist and full of juice. Mamma had given me 20 cents at the beginning of the trip to buy treats, and I spent it all on pears. One bite and juice would run down my face so I'd have to mop it off with my handkerchief. If the American food was all like that I'd be in heaven.

When the waves were quieter I went up to the deck to watch for birds and dolphins. There weren't any dolphins around and not many birds either. Everyone was too sick to play chess on the floor. The library was only for first class. I was almost starting to miss school and my friends back home.

I found a narrow ladder and went up to snoop. The door wasn't locked so I peered in. It was a small room with all kinds of instruments, covered with buttons and dials. There were little lights blinking on many of them, and dials with pointers. An officer spotted me and told me "Get lost, kid! We're piloting a ship here. No visitors."

Down on the deck I spotted one of the officers coming toward me, heading to the control room. He could see I was bored, I guess. "Hi, kid," he said. "Did you ever think how we can find our way on the ocean?" He talked slowly. It gave me time to figure out what he was saying.

"At school *il maestro* told us to look at stars," I said.

"OK—but look how cloudy it is. Do you see any stars, even at night last night?"

"Well, last night was a disaster," I said. "Very bad. I thought we were going down."

"Yes—the seas were a bit heavy for a while. But back to navigation. We have a very good compass, and we measure how fast we go in any direction. That way we can do the math and find out where we are on the charts. That's what they call navigation maps. Those charts even tell how deep the water is in many places, so we don't run into a shallow spot or a hidden island when there's fog. The depth sounder checks every hour. They've made charts of the floor of the ocean now. They learned a lot using radar the last few years searching for submarines."

I stood there with my jaw hanging as I tried to piece all those words together. I never heard of such a thing—roads on the ocean. "I'll tell you something else," he said. "Tonight at 7 bells—that's 11:30 ship time—we're going to pass our sister ship the *Vulcania*. It will pass to starboard, on our right, on its way back to Italy. You'll see the lights, and our ships will blink our lights at each other so we know we're both on time." I couldn't believe it—meeting a ship neatly out in the middle of the ocean—and being on time.

"Thanks, mister," I said.

That night when the bell rang six times, I slid down from my bunk, and stuffed myself in all the warm clothes I had. "What's going on?" the guy in the lower bunk growled. "Quit that noise. We're trying to sleep here. Maybe a slap will remind you to have more respect." He swung his arm at me but missed, then rolled on his other side and started to snore.

I scurried out, buttoning my jackets and pulling my hat over my ears, and climbed up to the right side of the deck, the starboard. I found a place to hide out of the wind and looked out to the ocean. It was black, no matter where you looked. You couldn't even see a star and a damp fog seemed to be over everything. Seven bells was the signal, he had said. I had to wait almost another half hour, but I wanted to be there in case the *Vulcania* was early. Suddenly far away on the right ahead of us I saw a tiny light. If I blinked it didn't go away. Little by little it seemed to get bigger, and finally, when the bell started ringing I saw a shape in the fog. There was a searchlight at the front and it started to blink at us. I saw a green light on its right front, and one also on the front starboard side of our ship. Their front light started blinking—on and off a few times—and then our front light blinked the same. That's how ships say hello.

### Chapter 8
# The Howling Atlantic

When we went down to supper there were paper streamers hanging along the walls in the dining room. Colored paper tablecloths on the tables were tucked under the rims on the sides, and balloons hung on the painted metal walls. "What's this—a party? What's going on?"

"It's New Years Eve," Mamma said. "Did you forget everything so fast? It is a big feast for Americans and we're starting here on the ship, now that we're on our way." It was a pretty good party. Musicians set up their instruments to play. We ate American food—roast beef and potatoes and green beans and crunchy lettuce salad with sweet red sauce on it. The grown ups got wine. I tried it but I didn't like it. It wasn't as good as my Nonno made, even when I mixed it with orange soda. There was apple pie and ice cream. The band started to play and people started dancing. Suddenly a big wave hit the side of the ship and a few bottles fell over. One of the dancers slid across and landed on Mamma's lap. The wind outside started howling. Then we were hit from the other side. We grabbed on to the tables as we pitched almost on our side. Back again to the other side, the drum and the drummer slid past me and landed against a tray of cakes. The cakes went flying, making it even harder for anyone to stand up on the frosting. Pretty soon the dishes were sliding over the rims of the tables and wine spilled everywhere. I really thought we would die and sink to the bottom of the sea.

Slowly and painfully we lurched back to our rooms, holding on to anything firm that we could find. We held on to the tables, to the bolted-down chairs, to the rails on the wall, to the door frames— anything. We crawled down the slippery pitching stairs and headed to our sleeping bunks. As we turned the corner toward the women's room, the ship rocked hard to the left. Mamma lost her hold on the handrail and fell, hitting her head hard on the steel corner. Blood started running down her face and she looked confused. "My mother's curse is coming true, Peppino," she mumbled.

"Curses are nothing but bad wishes, Mamma. You know wishes don't come true!" I tried to mop her off with my handkerchief, but the blood kept coming. We lived through a war and now she's dying in a hallway! Just our luck. I pulled on her and she finally staggered to her feet as I helped her through the door.

"No men in here!" a woman shouted, until she saw the blood. "*Dio mio!* (My God!) Here, put her on this bed. Get a wet towel!" I ran down to the sink at the end of the room and brought the towel. We wrapped Mamma's head tight and pretty soon the bleeding stopped. She looked up from under the towel bandage and mumbled something. I couldn't hear.

"*Cosa?*" I said. "What?"

"*Tu sei buon' com' il pane,* you're as good as bread." Tears came to my eyes as I realized I'd finally done something right—she was proud of me—I'd come through in a crisis. And the other passenger thought I was a man!

I returned to my bunk. People staggered in bit by bit. Pretty soon the roast beef, green beans, champagne and cakes started to come back up and people were filling those seasick buckets. The ride was choppy. The ship would tip so far one way that the ocean water completely covered my window and then the ship would turn the other way and I'd see we were out of the water. The lights on the deck were still on for the party. The ocean waves were taller than a house, splashing high on the side of the ship. There was snow in the air. Ice chips clattered on the windows, ringing on the steel of the ship. Bigger chunks of ice banged on the windows. It went on most of the night and I think a lot of people said their prayers who usually skipped them.

It finally quieted down when daylight started to glisten through the porthole. The engines were

still rumbling, so I knew we hadn't sunk. The grown
ups were sleeping, with their dress-up suits wrinkled
and spotted. I wanted to get to the bathroom before
the rush because I knew there would be lots of
emergency washing to do. I slid down from my bunk
and tiptoed through the long room. About halfway
there, I spotted a tightly rolled-up money bundle
against the wall near the door. I picked it up, hoping
it hadn't been thrown up on, and put it in my pocket.
Once I got back in my bunk, I opened it. It was a roll
of American money! No name on it. No clue of the
owner. A hundred and twenty-two dollars. Money
from heaven! A gift from the storm! I couldn't wait
to tell Mamma, but there were no boys allowed in
her room so I had to wait. When they rang 2 bells
for breakfast, I headed up to the dining room and
grabbed Mamma. "You'll never guess what I found!"
I squealed.

"*State zito,*" (Be quiet) she said. "What do you
have?"

"*Una fortuna—dollari Americani,*" (A fortune,
American money) I whispered.

"Not here—meet me on the deck, on the right
side near the chairs at the back at 4 bells. Oh, in case
you're interested, my head is better." Looking up,
I saw that she'd put band-aids over her cut and the
purple lump had gone down. You could hardly notice
it under her bangs. "Sorry," I said. "I was just so
excited about..."

"*Zito!* Quiet... meet me later!" I agreed, stuffed
the package deep into my pocket, and went inside to
eat a dish of hot oatmeal.

The dining room had been cleaned up pretty well. The stewards must have worked all night during the storm to have everything cleaned and washed. I wouldn't want their job!

At four bells I buttoned up my jacket and went up on deck. The air was clear and really cold—colder than I ever felt. That storm had really changed the weather. The waves were small. Seagulls were flying around the back of the ship where they throw off the garbage. They'll have a nice New Year feast. Plenty of garbage was made last night.

The deck was deserted, with most people sick or drunk or cold—maybe all three. Mamma came down the row of chairs bundled in her remade coat. "Let me see what you found," she said, and I showed her. "A hundred and twenty-two! *Dio mio!* Who has that kind of money to throw around? That's more than the cost of your ticket! Here, you can have $2 for yourself, and I'll save the rest. It will pay for your whole trip."

"But it belongs to somebody," I said. "Won't they be upset?"

"They didn't take care of it. Too bad. If there's a search and a person really needs it, we'll give it back." Later that day I saw the guy from Naples walking around the sleeping room looking carefully at the floor.

"Are you looking for something?" I asked.

"Mind your own business," he snapped. "Kids like you are too curious for their own good. Go back to the farm where you belong."

Maybe that's the money he got cheating the other card players. Mimmo and I had watched him ever since we boarded, playing *Scopa* with the other men on the deck. He'd slap down his cards and rake in their money, and a couple of times I saw him slip an extra card or two out of his sleeve or pants cuff. He'd chew down on his cigar and laugh at them. "It just isn't a good day for you, I guess. Too bad. You've found your master now." Off he'd go, rolling up their money into his pocket. Now who's the master, I thought.

*Chapter 9*
# L' America

Five days after the big storm, I noticed that the water was changing color—not so dark blue. If I looked carefully I'd see floating junk—a tire, pieces of wood, a couple of bottles. I saw different birds, not only the usual seagulls. I asked a steward and he said they fly out from the land. We were getting close! The next day the captain came to the loudspeaker and announced: "Tomorrow we will see New York. Have your baggage and personal things ready to leave the ship. We will have only 24 hours to have the ship cleaned and filled with food and fuel for the return trip to Italy. I ask your cooperation in these matters." Then he repeated it in Italian and Portuguese for the immigrants.

"Will Papá come to meet us?" I wanted to know. "How will he know where we are? How will he know me—I was only 14 months old when he went away. Does he have a car? How can we carry the mattress and sewing machine? What about the you-know-what (the money)? Do you think he'll like me?" I whispered the last words. I didn't dare say "Will you like him more than me?"

"You have too many questions, Peppino. Fathers always love their sons. We'll just do what we always do. Start at the beginning and work hard until we're done. That's what we always do and it worked before. Let's enjoy our last day at sea."

Well, that was a change. She wasn't the sort to enjoy for no reason. I wondered if she was worried about what our new life would be like in a new country, with a different house, different stores, different friends. I had grown taller this winter and was almost as tall as she, so I put my arm around her shoulder. She gave me an embarrassed look and shook herself. "Let's go on the deck and watch the birds," she said.

The next morning I woke up before dawn to the bellow of the ship's horn. I think it could be heard clear to Italy. Three big blasts. We had come up into New York harbor in the night, and the horn sent out the official message: We are here—send out the tugboats. I dressed fast and ran up to the deck. There was New York, still covered by twinkling lights in the dark winter morning. There must have been more than a hundred tall buildings! They were packed all together. I couldn't even see the streets from where I was. When I squeezed my eyes together I could see things moving, looking as small as ants. Then as we got closer I could see the streets with people and cars moving around. Far ahead I saw the Statue of Liberty. All along the sides were places to land ships and many of them were filled with ships of all sizes. Tugboats came up to the ship and two of them started to push us. Slowly they steered us toward the Statue of Liberty. As we got closer and the sun came up I could see men unloading the ships at the docks. They rolled out big barrels, huge boxes on carts, even a few cars. There were bins of fruit and oil barrels. People drove wagons and carts everywhere, transferring cargo to the waiting trucks. Carefully the tugboats steered us through the harbor and I thought we would park too, but we kept on going. We went past Ellis Island where Papá wrote was the place to be. But we couldn't get off! We were going to miss him! What if he was waiting for us on the island and we couldn't get off? I started to shout, "Help! Stop here! Let me off!" People on the deck laughed at me.

"You can't get off here—you'd have to swim!"

"But Papá is meeting us at Ellis Island!" I wasn't going to let them see me cry, but my heart sank.

Mamma came up on deck pretty soon, with a scarf wound around her hair, and explained. "We're not landing there this time. The captain said it is full, so we're going to Pier 17. They announced on the radio news that all passengers on *Saturnia* would be going through customs at Pier 17, so Papá will find out. One of his friends will call and tell him."

"Call? How can they shout that far?"

"There is a telephone at his cousin's house,

where he is staying. If there's a call, they'll get him
and let him talk on it. He'll find us." She didn't seem
concerned.

We sailed up the river until we saw a big sign
ahead, Pier 17, and the tugboats started to nudge the
big ship around so that the chains could be attached
to the pier. From a tug boat, a customs officer was
lifted up in a swinging seat and onto our ship. He
announced in three languages where to go: Surnames
A-E, Gate 1; Surnames F-J, Gate 2 and so forth.
We were B for Binetti so we had to aim for Gate 1.
We were to have our passports and visas ready to
show. We were to have all our property with us to be
inspected. Our families or friends would be waiting
in back of the barrier. It was funny to hear him say it
over in different languages.

"You stay here and watch for landing,
Peppino. I have to get our things together. I don't
want to lose that sewing machine!" I looked at
Mamma again—she looked different today. She had
her hair fixed in the beauty shop and was wearing
lipstick. Her red scarf was new and made her brown
eyes shine. I never saw her that way before. With
her fixed coat and everything she really looked
nice.

"Don't you want to be first to see Papá?" I said.
"You look pretty. He'll be watching for you."

"He's waited almost 10 years, he'll wait a
little longer," she said tartly. "Mattresses don't
grow on trees. Now go watch. Get down there near
the gangplank, but don't fall off!" Down she went
to see about our possessions and left me to look

for the father I had never met. Suddenly there was a loud thump and the ship vibrated. The engines slowed down and stopped. It was so quiet that my ears felt funny. They let down big chains with cables and clamped them around huge iron posts on the pier—two in front and two in back. It took two men each to carry them over to the posts. Big rubber bumpers kept the ship from scraping against the concrete pier. The tugboats tooted their whistles and left to find other big ships to park. I squeezed between the passengers until I was against the chain at the gangplank. I peered out at the crowd back behind the gates on the land, searching. There were so many faces and I didn't know a one. Until, yes, that's him! He looked exactly like the picture behind Mamma's candle. He was wearing a well-worn hat and a rumpled brown suit and a tie that didn't match. He had on a tan topcoat. He was smiling like in the picture. I'd know him anywhere.

As they lowered the gangplank, people crowded behind the chain pushing and shoving. As soon as the gangplank hit the pier, I jumped over the chain, ran down the gangplank and dashed across the waiting area. "Hey, kid—come back," they shouted. "You can't go there." In a blink I was a good 10 meters ahead of the chubby customs officer.

"Papá, Papá," I shouted as I threw my arms around him, knocking his hat sideways. "We're here. I found you. You're just like your picture!"

"Welcome to America, *figlio mio*." Over my shoulder he could see Mamma coming toward us, her red scarf waving in the wind and a big smile on her face. "Now we are a family again. How I've missed you both!" With an arm around each of us Papá hurried us through the customs line. Immigrants were lining up in long lines that curved around and out toward the door. He and I both had American passports, so we brought Mamma with us to the line that said "Citizens", where the agents were smiling and friendly. "Welcome to America, Missus," one said, and shook Mamma's hand. She stared in disbelief. Her experiences with officials had been different.

Outside, Papá waved at his cousin who drove up his Cadillac to load us in. I was in cars before, to take the mattress to Bari, and once in Naples, but this was an American car—big and heavy with a silvery statue on the front. Six people could fit in that car. I leaned back on the leather seat. "Life is good here," I said to Papá. I patted the smooth leather. "Life is good."

But when we got to our cousin's house, it wasn't a house. His family lived above their restaurant. Papá said it was a saloon—like a restaurant but mostly for drinking. That night it was noisy because those drinkers stayed up late, but the beds were comfortable and the house was really warm. No cold floors here. They were made of wood, with rugs that matched the walls. The big sons of the family were away at university, so there was room for all of us. Outside the window the green and yellow neon signs kept blinking and I could hear cars going by. But once my head hit the warm, soft pillow, I was gone.

*Chapter 10*
# New York

I awoke to see everything covered with snow —the cars parked in front of the tavern, the top of the neon signs. A streetcar clattered along the street very slowly while a man walked in front of it sweeping the snow off the track. Everything was quiet. Even the car horns seemed to honk softly. The city was asleep.

"Peppino," Mamma called from the hallway. "We have to get going. The train leaves for Chicago in two hours and we have to be on it—the tickets are paid."

"What about all our stuff—the mattress, the sewing machine—how can we get it on the train?"

"You cousin Cesare is getting it shipped. It will come to us in a couple of weeks. Papá has to get back to work. If he's not there, the candy batches will be late. They depend on him to make the right sugar and cocoa mix for the batch. He can't let them down."

I couldn't believe the size of Grand Central Station. It was so big inside it seemed our whole town could fit in it. We walked along quickly, across the huge marble hall that echoed the hundreds of voices, and down along one of the tracks until we found the car with a number matching our ticket.

"Here's our place," Papá said. "We have these two pairs of seats facing each other. You can sleep on one if you get tired."

I sat by the window to see what America looked like. It looked strange — all kinds of tracks and factories. Smoke poured out of the chimneys and we could look in the back windows of houses as we passed close. The steel wheels rattled steadily and the car rocked back and forth and made me sleepy. But just when I'd start to fall asleep with my head against the window, we'd go around a corner and the wheels would screech and bump and I'd wake up surprised. Mamma and Papá just sat, talking quietly. You'd think they would make more of a fuss after so many years in different countries, but they just sat there as if they had come in from trimming almond trees—tired and quiet. Mamma still had her red scarf on, and sometimes Papá would look over and smile a bit and pat her hand. She didn't pat back. "It's a new world, Gino," I heard her say. "It isn't home and never will be. What if we've made a big mistake?"

"Don't worry," he said. "Trust me—I won't let you down."

After about three hours it began to look

different out the window. America got flat, even flatter than our fields at home. We passed a lot of houses far apart with fields around them. I asked Papá why they were so far apart. "That's the way American farms are," he said. "People have their house and barn on their own land. Each one is like an island. They only go into town to buy things or go to church."

"They don't have a village?" I asked. "No *piazza*? How do they meet each other, or even find other people if they need them?"

"Americans like to be independent," he said. "The farmers take care of themselves, each family separately. It isn't like Italy where everybody teams up to do things. Here it's every man for himself. That's what they respect."

"Will it be that way in Chicago? All alone?" I could picture having no friends at all, and would have been happy to turn right around and go back. Who needs gold streets if you don't have any friends?

Papá peered down at me, as if he really saw me for the first time. He reminded me of Nonno. "You must miss your friends. In Chicago we'll be in a big city, in a part where most of the people are Italian too, and they live the Italian way. Kids play together outside and everyone walks around to the shops and to visit. Chicago isn't like these farms. You'll find plenty of friends there. Are you getting hungry?"

Of course I was. I was twelve years old and growing out of my pants every month. I could smell cooking from time to time in the train and wondered where it came from.

"There's a restaurant in another car," Papá said, "but it's very expensive and they only have American food. We'll buy something from the peddler who comes up and down the aisle instead."

Pretty soon a man came through the car pushing the food cart. I hoped for more of those big American pears, but all he had were apples and a pile of long yellow things I had never seen. Papá bought three apples and three of the yellow things. I bit into one and it was disgusting. I spit it out. Papá burst out laughing. I didn't think it was funny.

"Here, *figlio mio*, take off the outside. You eat the inside. It's called banana. Try another taste." He bent one end back and the thick yellow skin easily peeled off in strips. I took a bite. It was strange— sweet but not really juicy, sort of like pudding but firm. I had never had anything like it. It was almost as good as a pear.

So we had bananas for lunch, and apples for supper and I didn't even mind eating the strange food, I was so hungry. Papá said maybe we should try the dining car and get a dish of soup. Mamma said the ticket already cost enough and we'd eat tomorrow at our new home. Papá sighed and ate another banana.

In the morning I woke up with a sore neck from sleeping sideways in the chair. Papá was snoring leaning against the other window, and Mamma snuffled a bit in her sleep as she leaned on him. Her scarf had fallen off and her hair was messy and I thought to myself, this is my new family now. Mamma has Papá to lean on now and I'll be left out.

Everything is going to be different.

The rising sun was making long shadows on the snowy land. We were still passing farms. America must be all farms. There's nothing here. It's all empty. Every now and then we'd go over a bridge, or pass a town station. Sleepy people wandered out of their houses. Trucks that said "Milk" stopped here and there.

I quietly left my seat and went up the aisle to find the washroom. It was hard walking as the train swayed back and forth. After the bathroom there was a door toward the next car. I went through and could see the tracks going fast under my feet as I stepped between the cars. I opened the next car. So this is the fancy restaurant, I thought. There were small tables all along the sides with white tablecloths and tiny vases with a flower in each one. I watched a man in a nice suit carefully cut a thin piece of his bread and dunk it into an egg in a tiny cup. The coffee in his cup sloshed as we rolled along, and there was jam in a cut glass dish for his other bread on a silver plate. I never saw such a fancy breakfast before!

A waiter came up and spoke to me in English. "*Scusi?*" I said.

"Oh, another Italian. You're in the wrong car, child. Go back that way." He pointed back to the car I'd come from.

"I talk American," I said. "This is to eat?"

"Yes, to eat," he smiled. "Pay money. Eat." He pointed to his mouth and wiggled his fingers as if he was counting money. At least he talked slowly.

"OK," I said. "Go to Papá. Get money." I went back but I knew what the answer would be—"don't waste money we don't have"—so I sat down and waited for the banana peddler to come around again.

## Chapter 11

# Chicago

Once we got to Chicago, we took a taxi from
the LaSalle St. Station to Papá's apartment on Grand
Avenue. That station was really big too, but not as
fancy as the one in New York. Americans like things
big. Cars are big, stations are big, farms are big—even
streets are big. Maybe I could be someone big here
too—smart and rich. I said that idea to Papá and
he gave a strange smile. "It's not so easy, Peppino.
Everybody else wants to be big too, you'll see. Try to
be good and work hard. Bigness isn't everything."
I think he was getting me ready to see his house,
because it wasn't big at all. It wasn't even a house.
He lived upstairs over a grocery store, up a narrow
stairway with worn blue painted steps. Another
stairway in back took us up to his place on the third
floor. He unlocked the door and brought us in—to the

kitchen. Off to one side was the *salotto* that he called "living room." There was a big brown metal cabinet in the middle with a blue fire burning inside, and a metal pipe that went straight up to the ceiling, then across and out above the kitchen window. There were two bedrooms and the small one was for me, with a neat bed, a bookshelf, and a small metal desk with a light. In the kitchen there was a window that looked out on an empty space, across to another window where I could see a lady chopping vegetables. The small bathroom had thick, shiny, bumpy paint around the doors, so thick it was hard to shut the door. I wondered where Mamma would put the mattress and sewing machine. The main bedroom already had a mattress—I saw it.

"Here we are," he announced. "Just the right size for us, and we can buy food downstairs when we need it. You won't have to go to a market."

Mamma stared at him. "This is our house, Gino? Where can we store our supplies? Hang our washing? Dry tomatoes? We left behind a house with marble floors, a garden..." She looked ready to cry.

"Give it time, Lucia. *Pazienza.* (Patience.) It will be nice. Different, but nice. And we're all together. Peppino can go to a good school. *Paesani* (people from our town) live right on this street and the next one. Even the grocer downstairs is from our town. There will be plenty of old friends around here to talk to. We'll make it a home together."

She wiped her eyes. "I'll try, Gino. We've come this far and I promised. But it won't be easy..."

Once we unpacked, Papá took us on the

streetcar to Goldblatt's store for winter clothes. It
was so huge, bigger than even UPIM in *Via Sparano*
back home. Everything was organized in neat little
piles on shelves, ready for the clerk to get them down
and show them to you. All we had to do was point,
and a lady would bring down three or four things
to pick from. There were whole shelves of sweaters,
cabinets full of shirts, big racks of dresses. Mamma
asked for a lot of dresses to be shown but of course
she didn't buy any. She wanted to see how well they
were made. She was not impressed. "They'll fall apart
if you wash them," she told Papá. "When I make a
dress, it stays strong for years." The ladies grumbled
a bit when she shook her head No to each one.

"You're mighty picky," one said under her
breath.

"What's 'picky?'" I asked.

Papá explained picky meant a person like
Mamma who wanted everything just right, and for a
low price.

We did buy two things for me, though, so I
could use them for school. First, we got me rubber
overshoes. It's an odd thing. You put on your shoes
and then you put the boots on over them. I guess
you take them off when you come inside. I couldn't
think where a school would keep 20 or 30 sets of
wet rubber boots, but I thought the nuns must have
a plan. The other thing was a set of fuzzy ear covers
called earmuffs. I had never seen such a thing. Two
soft furry circles were attached to a wire. I had to
put the wire over my head so the fuzzy parts would
cover my ears. They were bright red and felt so good.

Papá said I could wear them going home because of the cold wind. I loved them from the start. It took a few days walking in slush before I loved my overshoes. We got a warmer jacket and hat for me to wear to school. Mamma said she'd make do with her remodeled coat and wear sweaters under it.

When we got home we were shaking with cold. Snow is pretty to look at, but not when it's coming down the back of your neck. That's when we were glad to have that heater in the living room and not a fireplace like we had in Italy. Mamma found a pan and made hot chocolate with cocoa powder and condensed milk, and we stood around the heater until our bones thawed out.

"Monday you'll need to go to Santa Maria Addolorata and sign Peppino up for school, Lucia," Papá said. "I'll show you tomorrow after Mass. You'll see where it is—the next block after the church. You can go early, before the students arrive. Sister Vittoria understands Italian. She's from *Abruzzo* herself, so she's hard to understand, but she'll help you sign the papers and find a class for Peppino." He turned to me. "You're on your way, my son. Study hard. Make us proud."

*Chapter 12*
# A New School

Walking into Santa Maria school early
Monday morning, the first thing that hit me was
the smell. It smelled like floor wax, and furniture
polish, and bananas, and wet wool all at once. The
black-capped valves at the ends of the radiators
hissed steam and were covered with chalk dust.
Every classroom we passed was filled with desks—six
rows with six in each row. Several rooms had folding
chairs lined up along the radiators under the window.
A wooden crate full of empty milk bottles stood
against the wall at the end of the radiators. There
were chalkboards and maps just like at home. Maybe
it's the same all over the whole world, I thought, and
wondered how it would be when all the kids arrived.
We walked down a long hallway with a shiny brown
floor, past a water fountain and a holy statue, to the

principal's office. My rubber boots left wet tracks along the shiny hall floor. Sister Vittoria stood up behind her desk and smiled. She had a round face and wore a long black habit. She had a veil over her hair just like the nuns back home. "Good morning," she said. "*Buon Giorno.* Shall we speak English?" She stopped for a bit and looked at us. We didn't say anything. Just looked at each other, confused. We didn't know what to say. "*Italiano? Vabbene— Italiano.*" She could do both! And shift back and forth! I could learn a lot from her.

Once she wrote down all our facts, Sister Vittoria peered at me over her rimless eyeglasses. "*Giuseppe... Peppino...* those are good names in Italy, but they won't do here. You'll be Joseph, maybe Joe. Watch my mouth and see how to say it. Jo—sef." I tried it. It made my mouth feel funny.

"That's right," she said. "Just practice. You have an American name now, and you've learned a new word of English. By summer, you'll be talking like a real American. That will open a whole new world for you. Now you've left Italian behind."

She wrote my name and address in her big record book and got Mamma to write her name in there too. "Get your books downstairs. There's a set you can borrow in the library. Take the rest of today off. Come tomorrow for Mass at 8 o'clock. School starts at 9. Lunch is from 12-1. You can go home to eat, and then we start again at 1 o'clock and work until 3. I am putting you into the immigrant class. You'll work only on learning English this semester, then next year you can join your regular grade level. It will not be easy for you—the other children have been working on English since September." I was glad she said all this in Italian—I could never remember it all if I had to translate.

She put her hands in her sleeves, gave a sort of bow to Mamma and said good-bye. That was it—I guess we'd pay later. If school was going to be this easy, I could get to like it here. We walked back down the hall and out the door, between long lines of kids coming in, marching to music that came out of speakers at the ends of the halls. They gave us funny looks, wondering why we were leaving when they were just coming in.

Next morning Mamma got me up early. After four *biscotti* and a big cup of milk with coffee, I packed up my borrowed books in our smallest suitcase and set out. Kids were coming down from the apartments all along the street, stomping in slush piles to splash each other and chattering away in English and about four different kinds of Italian. A couple of boys talked to me, and one was easy to understand. "*Sei Barese?* I asked. "Where are you from? What town?"

"*Sannicandro,*" he said. "*E tu?*"

"*So' da Bitritto,*" I replied. "I saw what happened in your town. All the people were dead in the church. Did your family die?"

"Just one cousin. We were lucky. We came to America as soon as we could get away. My name's *Vincenzo* but my American name is Jim."

Jim from Sannicandro—I had a new friend. "I'm *Peppino*—Sister said it's Joe in American. I have to learn English until June."

"We'll learn together, then. Sister puts us in teams to practice talking. If she hears any Italian, she waves her ruler at us."

"Does she hit?" I remembered my stinging hands from *Don* Cirillo in Bari.

"Naw. Never hits, just waves it around. She's like a nice mother. I think she likes us, but she tries to act tough."

"My mom is like that. Sounds really mean but she's softer than she thinks. I saw tears in her eyes once..."

That was the first of a long line of days, each one like the one before. Pray first, then try to read in English. Learn more words. Practice talking. Read more stories about saints. Write more words. Eat lunch. Play out in the street for a while, hitting a ball and chasing each other. Then more reading and talking. We learned about a million saints, and not much math. "Once you can talk, then the math will make sense," Sister said. "*Prima la lingua. La lingua controlla tutto.* (Language comes first. It controls everything.) Math will wait. Learn your words." And so we did, day after long day.

At Santa Maria we mostly played in the street after lunch. Carpenter School was public, two blocks away. It had swings and a big gray metal slide, polished down the middle by about a thousand butts sliding down year after year. They had a thing called a teeter-totter too, that you could balance up and down on. If the guy on one end jumped off, it would drop you hard on the cement causing lots of entertainment.

At our school stickball was the best game. Or it was the best if you knew how to hit the ball with a stick. Every American kid could hit that ball when someone threw it. All I could do with a stick was build a fire in a *braciere* and I missed the ball every time. "Hit that ball, Dago!" they'd shout. "Can't you do anything?" After a few days they didn't want me on their teams and pretended they didn't understand me when I asked. "No speaka, Dago. No speaka," they'd laugh and run over to play with other boys.

If I spotted Jim from Sannicandro, then we'd go together and ask. They couldn't pretend they didn't understand Jim. He got an A in English, which is like *lodevole*, the grade I used to get back home. Jim was good in other ways. By the end of the first week he introduced me to Vito, who came from Mola in 1947, and Carmi who was *Romano*. We practiced by ourselves with a ball and bat and we hit the ball about once out of five. One time the ball went over the high fence into the nuns' private yard and Carmi climbed over to get it and didn't get caught. After that our little gang got respect. Nobody ever dared go in the nuns' yard.

*Chapter 13*
# Working

By the time most of the snow had melted, Mamma was getting restless. "There's nothing to do here, Peppino," she told me. "No animals to tend, the water comes up in a pipe, the fire turns itself on, we can buy food downstairs. I'm going crazy."

"Remember on the train, how Mimmo's mother was going to sew and make money? Do you ever see her any more? Maybe she's keeping busy with that sewing job."

"I forgot all about her! I'll ask your Papá to find out from his friends where she lives. It would be nice to see somebody I know and hear a voice from home."

She found her all right—just over on Damen on the third floor. It was an easy walk. I heard them talking as I came into our kitchen from school. Mrs. DiNardi had taken a job at the factory that makes men's suits and was making good money sewing buttonholes on jackets. Every day she went on the streetcar to Hart, Schaffner & Marx, and all day she made buttonholes, buttonholes, buttonholes. She was hoping to get promoted to pockets, she told Mamma.

"And how is it to be back with your husband again," Mamma asked. "Are you happy together? What about the girlfriend?"

"We get along," Mrs. D replied. "The girlfriend was just a temporary situation. She didn't replace a wife and family. We don't talk about her."

"Does he ever talk about the days he was here with Gino?" Mamma hesitated.

"You suspect Gino? That's a laugh. Gino is as faithful as a dog. You shouldn't worry. All they used to do is play *bocce* and drink beer at the club."

"You're sure? He doesn't say much about those years."

"Just get a job. That's what Americans do. Everybody gets a job. The wives get their own money. Then you have money for things you like, furniture covers, new drapes, maybe a car. You don't have to ask permission."

At supper Mamma brought the matter up to Papá. "I think I should get a job, Gino. Grazia works at a suit factory and she's going to get new drapes with the money. Imagine, she gets paid for just making buttonholes. I can do that with my eyes closed. The money would come in handy."

"It's the man's duty to support his family," he objected. "What will people think if my wife has to go out to work? They'll think I can't take care of my family. I'll look like a failure."

"It didn't bother them when I was pruning grapes and harvesting olives, did it? That was work. How about hauling water and raising rabbits in the basement. Wasn't that work? I almost died in the war doing everything to survive. Sewing won't hurt me. If your friends are jealous that I get to have my own money—that's too bad. They told us America was 'land of the free' so I think I'm free to make money. And I'll find a job for Peppino too, so we'll all make money and move away to a better house."

Papá's face fell. "So that's it—you don't like our house, do you. I know it's small. It was fine for me, but I can see that it's a big change from our home in Italy. Go ahead if it makes you happy." He drooped his head as he turned away. Maybe he's not so happy to have us all here, I thought. It's more complicated.

Once Mamma was at the factory every day, I had lots of time on my hands after school. As long as I was home in time to heat up the pasta water, I could wander around and learn the neighborhood. Sometimes I went with Carmi and Vito to watch kids' teams play baseball. What a boring game—they just stood around most of the time waiting for the two or three people actually doing something. Soccer is what they need, I thought. Get everybody running around at once and put a bit of life in it.

If only Dominic were here we could get a

game going. I remember how he kicked that ball and knocked Sgt. Thorton's hat off. For a minute that day we thought we'd get shot—knocking off an officer's hat—and then he turned out to be such a good guy. And the day we cheated the Nazis by giving them empty eggs – those were the days. We never did get shot at all, and we had a lot of laughs. Now we're supposed to be interested watching baseball—it's like watching olives grow.

One day we tried to sneak into a movie like we used to do back home, but we got caught and the guy called the police. The cop was big—not exactly fat, but you could see he didn't miss any meals. He had red hair like Sgt. Thorton, so I thought maybe he was English. I asked him, "English, sir?" and pointed to him.

"Saints preserve us! English! Not a bit of it, they drove us into the sea. You couldn't pay me to be English." He got red in the face and kept tapping his club on his other hand.

"*Scusi*, sorry. I only come now from Italy," I said. I didn't want to offend a man with a big club.

"New here then, are you? I'll forgive you then. This is the American rule: you have to pay to get in the movie. I don't care what Dago rule you had before. Pay first and there'll be no trouble. *Capeesh?*" I understood "pay" and his messed-up word for *capisce*.

"OK, Sir. Pay first, OK?" He nodded. We ran off toward home with Vito in the lead by half a block.

## Chapter 14
# Summer Jobs

"We need to find you work for the summer," Mamma announced one Saturday morning. "You're old enough to earn your way, and there will be three months without any school. Maybe your Uncle Carlo will know of street builders that need a water boy. He just arrived in America and is working on the streetcar tracks downtown."

"Uncle Carlo is here? How did he do that? Didn't he have to get a visa like you did? I thought he was messed up from the war and taking care of Nonna Paola."

"He said he paid a *padrone* (contractor, boss) to smuggle him in to work on the streets. He said it was easy. Now he has a job. Maybe he can get you one too."

All right, I thought—not so different from

picking up rocks in our fields. I can do that. "*Si,*
Mamma," I said. "But do they hire kids? None of my
friends has a job."

"You can be the first, the leader. We just have
to make you look older." She found Papá's old shirt
and pants and hat and put me in them. "Hmm—you
need some beard." She wiped her hand over the vent
of the heater where it was a bit scorched and it came
away grayish. She rubbed my cheeks a bit. "There, if
they don't look too close they'll think you're sixteen.
Stand up tall but pull the hat over your eyes." She
leaned back and squinted. "You'll pass. Just say
you're sixteen and you are willing to work hard. Walk
down Grand Avenue toward the lake until you find
the road crew and just ask the boss. Here's ten cents
for the streetcar if you come home tired."

I walked down the street about a mile until I
saw where the tracks were being torn up. Men were
taking out the bricks of the street and re-setting them
to be level. Another group were putting the tracks
down after them, pounding spikes down into the
street between the stones. I saw Uncle Carlo down at
the end swinging a pick to get the next set of stones
out.

He looked tired and sweaty. "*Zi' Carluccio,*"
I hollered. He looked up and waved me over. I told
him what Mamma had said. He set down his pick and
tapped the next man.

"I go see boss," he said, and led me over to a
man with a big cigar and no tools in his hands. "You
need help, boss?" he said.

"Not hiring now. Sorry."

"He's a good work'. He's a strong. Maybe

water boy?"

"Nope. No kids. Get back to work, Bellino. I don't pay you to stand here talking."

"Go home Peppino," Uncle Carlo said. "Tell your mother she has to wait until you grow up more. She's a push you too much. She's a push everybody. Too much push. You just a kid." He gave me a gentle push toward home, mopped his face with a big handkerchief, and picked up his pickax.

Mamma wasn't too pleased. "Did you ask nice? Doesn't he see that you're strong? Next week we'll try another job." Next week came and the man at the shoe factory said the same thing—no kids. Same story with the remodeler fixing a store around the corner. Goldblatts didn't need clerks, and the movie house didn't need ushers. I had about given it up and thought I could have a nice vacation all summer, until two weeks later Mamma announced at supper, "I found the perfect job for you Peppino! The grocery store downstairs needs a beginner helper."

"What do I have to do?"

"You do whatever they tell you—sweep, pile up vegetables, throw out garbage, climb up to get cans off the high shelf, carry groceries for people—just do what they tell you."

"Do they pay me?"

"Not much, but you'll learn a lot. Three dollars a week will help the family. You can keep a quarter for the movies."

So I took the grocery store job. Every day after school for two hours and eight to four on Saturdays. It was a job to do what nobody else wanted to do. After three weeks I was sick and tired of climbing up and down for heavy cans and hauling bags of groceries up the stairs for people who ordered on the phone. I complained to Vito and Carmi. "But you're getting paid," they said. "You're making money anyway." We didn't hear Jim from Sannicandro complaining because he was never around. His mom made him take care of his two younger brothers and she didn't even pay him. But Vito had an angle. "My dad knows a peddler named Aiello," he said. "He sells things from his horse cart that goes up and down the alleys. He told my dad he needs helpers for the summer."

That sounded a lot better, almost like my business I had in Italy. I thought Vito and I would be selling vegetables, but Mr. Aiello had another plan. Next to his garage was a huge round cement tank, almost 10 feet high and about 6 feet across. Our job was to put on big rubber gloves, climb up the ladders on the outside, pour in gallons of strong chemicals, and then fill the tank with the water hose. Then we'd climb down and fill up gallon jars under the spigot to sell. That stuff smelled awful. It burned our eyes. We had to be careful not to touch our face with the gloves. One time I pushed my hair out of my eyes. I got a light patch like a skunk on my front hair and my eyes hurt for days.

Once the bottles were filled, we loaded them on his cart and went through the alleys yelling "Link-ammonia." Women came out on their porches and called down an order. Mr. Aiello sent us up with the bottles and we brought back the money. He kept the cash, marking every sale in a grubby wrinkled notebook that he kept under his seat. At the end of the week we got 10 cents for every bottle we sold. He often had vegetables too, on the other side of the cart. If there were beat-up ones left at the end of the day, he gave them to us to use them up. Mamma made good soup with them. We ate a lot of soup.

We shared the alley routes with the "rags ol' iron men" who collected any kind of cloth or metal to be re-sold. They collected broken irons, fencing wire, all kinds of cloth from rugs to underwear, pots and pans, paint cans, broken gutters, broken bicycles. I wanted to get one of those bicycles and fix it but most were completely smashed. There was a lot of action in alleys, with kids playing, horse carts delivering or selling, sometimes a dog fight or a cat up a tree— always something. Once school was out we worked for the peddler full-time.

I was worried about Mamma though. She didn't feel good and sort of drooped around. Often she didn't want to cook or even eat. She was slowing down. One day she came home from the suit factory and told me and Papá she was quitting. "I have to go to a doctor, Gino. I feel a hard lump here in my belly. Something is wrong with me, I know." Papá asked among his friends how to find a doctor, and finally found one who spoke Italian. The appointment was two weeks away and a cloud of gloom settled on our family. I didn't think Papá and I could run a whole family by ourselves. Mamma always organized us.

Finally she went to the doctor and came home looking very sad, sadder than I had ever seen. We sat down at the table. "What did you find out," Papá asked.

"The doctor says *tumore*, Gino. *Il cancro.*"

"*Impossibile!* You just came here. You lived through the war, all those bad times." Papá looked ready to cry. He reached for her hand. "But you can't die. They can do operations here. A woman in the office at the candy factory had an operation and she lived. She got better and came back to work. We'll get you an operation and you'll get better."

"You know we don't have money, Gino. It's just my cross. It can't be helped. My next move will be the cemetery."

"It isn't your cross until we try everything, Lucia. You've never given up before. You're not moving to any cemetery. You can't give up now. We'll find a good doctor that can do an operation." Papá sounded hopeful. Maybe a *tumore* could be fixed in America. They fix lots of other things. He knew so many friends. Surely there would be one who knew of a good doctor.

"Maybe I can find another job," I volunteered, "work on Sundays too. That might help."

"It doesn't actually hurt yet, so I'd better cook your dinner," she said. She put on her apron and took down a jar of tomato sauce. I put the plates out. Papá cut the bread. We all looked like we were at a funeral. Until we could find the surgeon, it was going to be a sad time. When Carmi called me from downstairs to come out and play, I told him I was busy.

*Chapter 15*
# New Arrival

Dominic showed up one morning—Dominic from Italy, my old friend Dominic who dared the Nazis. The bell rang early on a Saturday morning just as I was getting my eyes open enough to get up and go to work. Mamma went to the door and let out a shriek. "What are you doing here? How did you come here? *Che cos' ha fatto?*" (What have you done?) Are your family with you?" I could hear her rapid-fire questions through the bedroom wall, and Papá's footsteps as he rushed down the hallway to the door. They pulled Dominic inside and we all crowded around him and hugged him.

He was taller than last December, and skinnier than I remembered. He set down his duffel bag. With everyone talking, in Italian of course, I finally got his story straight. He saved up every penny until he could get a train ticket to Naples. He sneaked out of his house and didn't look back. He hung around the docks and made friends with sailors, telling them sob stories about his sick mother in America, his little baby sisters that were going hungry. Maybe he told about their hungry dog too, if I know him. He could lie better than anyone I knew. He convinced a sailor to smuggle him on board when they were about to leave for America, and just slept around on the ship wherever he found an empty space, always pretending to be lost on the way to his cabin. A girl asked him to sit at her table, until her mother found out and shooed him off. In New York he walked off the ship with the crew as they were putting the big bales of garbage out. He thumbed his way, riding in cars and trucks all the way to Chicago. Now he was in our front room, hungry and needing a bed.

"You can stay here for a while, Dominic," Papá offered. Mamma didn't look too happy. "You can sleep on the mattress my wife brought from home. We can roll it out here on the floor near the heater every night."

Mamma glared. "We're all busy every day and there's no garden. We have to buy everything. You'll have to help out. *Chi dorme non piglia pesce.* (If you sleep you catch no fish.) You can sleep here on the couch for a couple of weeks anyway, until you get *sistemato.*" She looked sideways at Papá. "My mattress doesn't belong on a floor."

We had a lot to say to each other, but about half an hour later Mamma reminded me. "You have work to do. Aiello will be expecting you. You can talk all night once the work is done. Tomorrow too. Papá and *Zi' Carluccio* are going out to gather *cardoni* (cardoons, wild edible plants) and dandelions after Mass. You boys can go with them and help.

After Mass on Sunday we changed into working pants, gathered our sacks and knives, and set out. The streetcar rattled along through neighborhoods all the way out to the end of the line. The air seemed fresher there and I could see a big woods ahead of us.

We got out and walked. The houses there were as big as our house in Italy, and each one had grass and flowers around it. A few had a fenced garden with tomato plants started, but nobody had a good strong wall like we had at home. We headed for a place Papá knew. Houses had not been built there and there was a big area of dandelions and other wild plants. Mamma wanted *cardoni* with big heavy stalks like rhubarb that she could cook first and then cut into pieces to fry. The dandelions would make great salad.

As we walked along, I noticed that kids playing on the sidewalks grabbed their toys and headed inside. Probably time for lunch, I thought. Then one of the women looked out her door, screamed and grabbed her kids inside, slamming and locking the door. We looked at each other, puzzled. "They couldn't be afraid of us, we're taking weeds. Do we look like Nazis?" Dom asked. "Those kids look terrified."

"I think it's our old clothes and the knives," Papá said. "They always do that. I tried to talk to a lady one time and tell her how good *cardoni* are, but she shook her head at me and hurried off. Americans are funny that way. They are easily scared by dirt and strangers."

Zi' Carluccio just said sadly, "I don't think we belong here. We should go home."

"No, Carlo. You just need to find a nice girl to marry, fill out the papers and become American. Then you'll fit in. At least in our neighborhood..." We kept walking, dragging our big burlap bags along the sidewalk. "Pick up your bag, Peppino," Papá said. "If you wear holes in it, the food will fall out and get dirty."

The men kept talking. "I'm not looking for a girl, Gino. I survived the war," *Zi' Carluccio* said. "I don't know if I can survive a wife."

I started to laugh but Papá poked me with his elbow. *"Non si' scherzan', Peppin'!* (Don't mess around.) Your uncle has been through a lot. Go over across the street and find us a batch of *cardoni*. Look for the ones with the thick stems."

Papá knew that Uncle Carlo had sneaked in just like Dominic. I'd heard him and Mamma talking when they thought I was asleep. When they talked so soft, I knew it was worth listening. Mamma was worried that he'd get arrested. Papá thought if he kept his head down and didn't get in trouble, he'd be OK. I wasn't so sure. In our neighborhood everybody noticed what everybody else was doing. It's as if there were eyes on the buildings. Uncle Carlo was sure to be noticed, I thought.

Dominic and I went down the street, inhaling

the sweet smell of the just-cut grass as we passed the yards. This neighborhood smelled so good, like grass and flowers and a bit of gasoline. If there was wood smoke too, I'd think I was back home it Italy. As we got close to the woods we saw a big empty field. We found plenty of plants we didn't know there, American plants, and almost in the middle a big area of late June *cardoni*, strong and juicy. We cut a whole burlap bag full while Papá and Uncle Carlo concentrated on dandelions for salad. All the way home in the streetcar we were quiet, each thinking his own thoughts. Mamma would be pleased, I thought, to have all this good food just growing out there, free for the taking. They weren't weeds to her. Maybe she could find a wife for her brother, too. She always came through when she put her mind to it.

*Chapter 16*
# Summer News

Summer in Chicago was hot and wet and sticky. Papá and I came home sweaty and crumpled to find Dominic outside practicing pitching pennies or kicking a ball around by himself. Mamma would be sitting in the steamy kitchen fanning herself with a cardboard fan I made out of a box from the grocers. "*Vien'a' mangia'* (Come and eat)," she'd say grumpily. "It's ready." We had an electric icebox to keep things cool, but we knew cold drinks would harm our stomachs, so we washed the pasta down with warm water or orange soda with wine in it. If there was a breeze, we'd sit outside on the flat roof between our apartment and the one at the back. I don't remember it being so hot at home, or maybe I wasn't paying attention, but the Chicago summer was pulling Mamma down.

In the middle of July I came home to find that Mamma had her sewing machine out in the middle of the front room. There were pieces of cloth and patterns all over the couch and the top of the turned-off heater. It looked as if she was making us all undershorts, but when I looked close the patterns were very small. And strangely, she was humming to herself and smiling. "*Cos' è?*" I asked. "What's going on?"

"I went to the other doctor today. I don't have *un tumore*, I have *un bambino*."

"Don't joke with me Mamma. It isn't funny." I looked again. Sure enough, she was happy and she had pieces of baby clothes all around her. "You're serious, Mamma? A real *bambino*? Did you tell Papá?"

"He knows. He went to the doctor with me and then back to work. He had to finish cooking that batch of peppermints for the Christmas market so they can ship next month. But he's happy. After all this time, he'll see his child grow up in his company. He missed all those years with you."

That bit of news changed a lot of things. For one, Mamma was so happy, happier than I've ever seen her. She sang when she was cleaning the house. She made tiny shirts and gowns and stuff. Once in a while I'd see her, when she thought no one was watching, rub her stomach and smile. Papá was happy too, whistling when he got home even when he was tired. He liked to sing along with the opera program on the radio. He smiled at Mamma a lot.

The only problem was the heat. We were cooking alive in the apartment. Even after we decided to freeze ice and put it in our drinks, the heck with our stomachs, we were still hot. One day Papá came home with something new. He called it a fan, and it was a machine with flat things that spun around, blowing the air. He tied four strips of cloth to the front, and when he turned the motor on, they flew straight out to warn us to keep our fingers away. It was nice to sit in front of it and just feel the air. He put it up on the turned-off heater so it could blow on Mamma while she sewed.

The other new thing we got was a phone. Papá was worried about Mamma being alone all day with the American *bambino* coming. The man from Illinois Bell showed up one day in his truck. He installed wires from the downstairs grocery store up along the wall to our house, and through a drilled hole to the inside. On the wall next to the place for the phone he put a metal box with a slot to put nickels in. It had a lock on it and he explained that he'd come once a month on the third Thursday around noon to open the lock and take out the nickels. Then he'd change them for other money and give us back the nickels in a dish to use when we had to make calls. It took me a while to explain all this to Mamma. She didn't see why he wanted money when he had the nickels. She was happy to have it though. Her friend Rita had a phone, and there was one downstairs in the store, so she could call them if she needed to. I think she was beginning to like America.

*Chapter 17*

# Becoming American

By September I was glad to go back to school and get organized. Summer had been crazy, with different jobs all over the place. It wasn't only the selling in the alleys. I worked a few Saturdays in a shoe factory, polishing heels on a machine.

Carmi had found a job for both of us at Riverview, selling balloons on weekends. It paid pretty good, ten cents for each helium balloon we sold. It was tricky filling up the balloons from the big pressure tank, though, and if we broke one we were docked ten cents, so a lot of times we about came up even. As we walked up and down the sidewalks outside Riverview, I could see people going in to have fun and I wanted to go too. From the street I could see tracks that went up high and then down like a tall hill. People screamed every time their train car went over the top. Some of them came out eating big piles of pink fluff on a stick and the kids' faces were smeared and sticky when I handed them their balloons. They weren't sticky enough to hang on to the strings though, and often the balloons sailed up and away leaving the kids crying for another one. I was surprised that a few parents even bought a second balloon just to shut them up. They should have a mother like mine I thought. They wouldn't even get the first one.

Finally I convinced Mamma that I should keep enough of my pay to go one time into Riverview, "so I could understand my job better," I told her. We told our boss we needed an hour off and he said OK. I should have known better than go in with Carmi, though.

The month before at Navy Pier, we were just messing around playing along the edge of the pier that extended far out into Lake Michigan. We were tagging each other and running around. Carmi gave me a big push and I landed in the water. It was deep, so deep my feet couldn't touch the bottom. I screamed for help. He thought it was a joke. The water filled my mouth and I struggled to get a breath. I tried to hold my face out of the water, but I kept going up and down. I couldn't swim and thought I was going to die. No matter how hard I pumped my arms and my legs I couldn't keep my face above the water. I had never learned to swim. I was swallowing water and couldn't get air. I couldn't shout, all I could do was sink. Everything went quiet as I lost my battle.

Vito jumped in and pulled me up.

They laid me out on the pier and started pumping the water out of me. I was coughing and choking, but finally they got me breathing.

I was glad of Vito that day. Vito grew up in Mola, a fishing town, and probably could swim as a baby. He said kids there know how to swim under the fishing boats to free the nets when they're caught. Nobody in our town could swim and nobody ever wanted to. A bathtub was deep enough, if we had one.

We walked home slowly all the way to Grand Avenue to let my clothes dry out in the sun. Carmi never said sorry. I never told Mamma.

Anyway, into Riverview we went, Carmi in the lead. We bought tickets for the Bobs, the Tunnel of Love and the roller coaster. We rode through the tunnel on the boat and everyone yelled to hear the echo. Not any love that I could see. Then we went on the Bobs, up and down fast, leaving my stomach up in my throat. After we staggered around a while, Carmi said the roller coaster was next, so we did that too. I was almost getting used to having my stomach up there. "We have enough for two more rides," Carmi said. "I dare you to ride down the parachute."

A parachute was rigged up to run down on a wire so the landing was set, but nothing but air held it up as it dropped. It looked just like what we had seen soldiers use in the war. And it looked like about a thousand feet up. "C'mon. Even little kids can do it. You just ride down."

He was right. There were a lot of kids doing it. There was a sign, though, that said you have to be twelve and that the owners would not be responsible for any accidents. I thought some more. Probably I won't really die. If I break my legs I won't have to go to school. I didn't see any people lying injured at the bottom. "OK, Carmi. If I go on the parachute will you give me what you earned today?"

"Only what I sold for one hour."

"One hour is peanuts. Two hours' worth."

He took the bet. We went over and gave our last tickets to the operator. He put us on a wooden seat attached to the parachute and laid a bar across our laps. "Hold on, boys," he said. He didn't have to tell me twice. I had a grip on the seat frame like my life depended on it. The operator pushed a switch and the parachute started to go up. It went up slowly, and as the ground got farther and farther away Carmi started to mess around. He shifted his weight back and forth, making the seat swing. "La, la, la—here we go up to the sky," he chanted. "Isn't this wonderful, Peppino?"

I was afraid to look down. Every time the seat moved I felt like I would go down and crash. I tried to keep my eyes closed. But then I peeked. We could see the weathered tops of the booths, all the rusty marks on the tops, the heads of people walking, the machinery that runs the rides. I could hardly breathe. My fingers were wrapped around the frame so tight I couldn't let them go. There was no frame between us to hold so I grabbed Carmi's leg. "Hey, let go. That hurts..." His voice was lost in the wind as the clamp suddenly let go of the parachute and down we went, fast. I opened my mouth to take a breath and suddenly we were down, hitting softly on the target painted on the blacktop.

The operator opened the bar and we staggered off. "Back to work," Carmi shouted. "Last one to the balloon stand is a rotten egg." If I was an egg, I thought, I wouldn't have wasted my money to be scared to death. Americans must be crazy to think this is fun. But at least I won the bet and wouldn't have to confess to Mamma.

*Chapter 18*
# Back to Work

The summer ended too fast and in no time it was time to go back, now into 8ᵗʰ grade with the regular American kids. It felt funny at first, talking English all the time. I made plenty of mistakes, especially when they weren't talking about saints. But every day I learned more words. I got the nice ones in class and the rough ones on the playground. They still called me "Dago" but I didn't care. Almost half the class were Dagoes of some kind, either new ones or older ones who could talk better. Soon we'd be a majority.

Mamma started going to school too. Chicago Commons gave lessons in English to new people and Mamma was determined to learn to "talk American" so she could keep up with the new baby as he grew.

She planned to get her citizenship too. "It's better to go to school now," she said. "When I was young I couldn't go. No girls got school after 4ᵗʰ grade. I'm going to do it now while I have a chance." So every Thursday it was my job to clean up after supper so she could go the four blocks to the lessons. She talked to me, trying her English. It sounded so funny to hear American sounds coming out of my mother's mouth. They didn't teach about saints at Chicago Commons, so we didn't have the same set of words. She learned "grocery" and "phone bill" and I knew about "martyrs" and "holiness". If it was important, it had to be in Italian so we'd really understand. Listening to us, Papá just shook his head.

I found a new job too. No more grocery store. I was moving up to the butcher shop. Every day after school I'd go for two hours and move meat in the walk-in refrigerator, sort out the good bones to sell from the scrap bones, clean shelves, wash knives and deliver orders. I was learning to take orders through the phone too. "*Pronto*" I'd say. "What'cha wan'?" Then they'd tell me in Italian, I'd pass the word to Mr. Martino, and then I'd have to take the package down the street to deliver. They'd usually give me an extra quarter to keep. I didn't mention that to Mamma when I turned over my pay envelope. *Silenzio,* I thought. It works in America too.

Saturdays were more interesting. The shop opened at 9 o'clock, so I went at 6 AM to learn the meat-cutting trade. First I'd help the butcher carry the big cold beef quarter out of the walk-in cooler and put it on a big butcher's block. Then for three hours Mr. Martino would show me how he could take a quarter of a cow and carefully trim it into pieces of meat.

That cooler was a whole room cold as an icebox. There was one light hanging in the middle, and half carcasses of pork, beef and lamb hanging on big hooks from the ceiling. Vito came over one day and went in with me. He liked the echo. Sometimes he'd get me to let him in so he could practice his voice lessons and listen to himself. He tried to sound like Mario Lanza. He wasn't even close. That only happened when Mr. Martino was out at the bank or having lunch with his wife upstairs.

To cut the meat, first Mr. Martino would hone his big knife on a steel file, up one side, down the other, keeping the knife almost flat. Zip, zip, zip—up and down fast. It was amazing that he never hit his own hand. He was so fast and strong. He'd make a careful slice down below the ribs to separate the loin section and the ribs. He'd turn one around and say, "Here, see these are the ribs. We just slice along here... and here..." He'd grab the big heavy cleaver and chop, chop, between the bones and there was a rib steak. It was amazing to watch, and every week he'd let me do a little more. "Don't be fast. Be right. I don't want to have to make those pieces into hamburger," he'd say. He showed me just where to put the knife point, where to slice straight, where to chop. Then at five minutes before nine, he'd take all the knives and wipe them off, put on a clean apron, and send me to work in the back cleaning feathers off chickens, killing rabbits, washing bins. I learned how to make Italian sausage, squishing the ground meat mixture through a funnel into long tubes made from pig intestine. Now and then I'd do a delivery. My lessons were private, a favor to my parents to get me ready for a lifetime job.

He let me weigh out the orders too, and I got to talk to all the neighbors. One morning a man came in wearing an expensive suit and smoking a cigar. I didn't know him. Mr. Martino bent down and whispered in my ear, "Give him whatever he wants. Free. Be very polite." Then he slipped around the corner into the back room. Free, I thought, why free? But I did what I was told.

"You new here, kid?" the man asked, looking around. "Where's the boss?"

"He said to give you our best," I told him. "No charge. Does he owe you or something?"

"Yeah," he laughed. "He owes me all right. Just cut me three of those rib steaks and about three pounds of round steak. Make the round steak thin. My wife is going to make *bracciole* for my birthday." He puffed on his cigar blowing smoke all over the counter and seemed to be thinking. He smiled to himself. "He owes me. Yeah. That's a good one." I cut three beautiful steaks off the big piece, with fine, white lines like marble. They would be tender. I slapped them down on the big waxed paper and wrapped them up fast, tying the package with thin string from the big spool over the counter. Then I did the same with the round steak, making them as thin as I could without slicing off my own finger. I passed over the wrapped packages.

"Thank you for your business," I said politely. He looked down through narrowed eyes. He reminded me of the flour seller at the *Borsa Nera* during the war. "You got class, kid," he said. "Class and guts." He took his packages and walked out.

Mr. Martino came quietly out of the back room. "You did good. You know who that is?"

"No. Just a smoker. It stinks in here."

"That smoker is the *capo* around here. Everybody owes him, if we don't want trouble. He's the guy to see if you have a problem. That's Mr. Beretta. You don't need to know any more. Better that way."

"He's trouble, but he helps? That doesn't make sense."

"Didn't you just come from Italy? Remember the Fascists?"

"Remember them? I remember that they took our house."

"But they built the water system too, right?"

"Well, yes. But they were mean and they pushed everybody around."

"There are people like that everywhere, Peppino. Just give them what they want and stay out of their way. You last longer that way. Now let's get those chickens cleaned for Mrs. D'Amico and you can run them over to her."

We went back to work, dipping the dead chickens in boiling water and then tumbling them over and over in the machine with rubber "fingers" to

take off the feathers. We took the insides out of each
one, washed them and wrapped them up. "You can
have one to take home, Peppino," Mr. Martino said.
"Don't mention this visit to your parents. It would
only worry them. Your father always worries about
the Black Hand, but we're doing OK here. I just have
to play it careful."

Walking along later I kept thinking. We got
away from the Nazis. The Fascists lost. We got free
of all that. We came all the way here. And now I find
the same kind of people are shopping in my butcher
shop. It's like the same thing all over again. I just
hoped that *capo* didn't have an army.

*Chapter 19*
# New Jobs

Sitting around the table after dinner Sunday, I heard Uncle Carlo lower his voice to Mamma. Lower voices often say interesting things, so I was very quiet as I dried the dishes. "Lucia," he said. "I had a job offer yesterday."

"About time," she replied. "Digging in the street is beneath you. Hard on your back too. The war took a lot out of you. Did you take the job?"

"I'm not sure, Lucia. It was a strange offer." He stirred his coffee again and looked down. Mamma pulled over a chair and sat down, rubbing her back.

"And so?"

"You know the guys who meet in back of Gianni's Restaurant? They play poker in the back room and always seem to have a lot of money in their pockets to gamble with?"

"I heard about them. I don't go into restaurants." I could see her face getting her hard look. "Don't look for trouble, Carlo."

"I was just there getting a sandwich, and this Silvestro, his American name is Little Sammy, walked over to me and said, 'I need some muscle.'

'Go the fish store,' I told him. 'It's down the street that way.' I pointed outside. I thought he wanted to buy *cozze*. Americans call them mussels.

"He gets a real mad face and says 'You some kinda wise guy? You got a smart mouth. Somebody gonna shut it for you.' He goes and sits down. Don't look at me no more.

"I don't know what he's mad about, so I ask Mr. Salerno. He's a laugh. 'It's muscle, Carlo, *forza*, not shellfish. That's what they call the strong guys that work for them. They drive trucks, deliver beer and packages. Mostly they work at night. Sometimes they hit people who make trouble, beat 'em up a bit. Show 'em who's boss. You know, just teach 'em a lesson. They break windows if people owe money. Break their car. They follow orders.' I don't like this kind of job, Lucia. It's too much like the army and I didn't like the army. What do you think? Should I take it?"

"I think they're trouble, *Carluccio*. I am your older sister, and I advise you: stay away from them. So much money around in dark rooms means only one thing. They're not honest. Nobody gets all that cash by being honest. And what if the police find you working for them? They'll send you right back to

Italy. No. If that Sammy asks you again, say you have a job. Thank him. Bow and smile and act like you were so honored. Then get away."

Uncle Carlo nodded slowly. He shook his head. "It was good pay, Lucia. I hate to lose it. But you're right. Those jobs don't sound right. It may be only business but I don't want trouble. I'll keep on digging. There are always more roads to fix in Chicago."

As I listened, I kept thinking. Dom said he had a new job too. It was as a messenger. He'd take envelopes from the guys at Gianni's and deliver them to people. I asked him last week why don't they put them in the mailbox? "They're too thick, Peppino. And too important. I think there's money in them, or maybe secret letters. I asked once and they told me I don't need to know. So I play dumb, I don't say anything, but they pay me good. It's $10 each message." Leave it to Dom to find a good job. Here I was working every day and all day Saturday for $10 and he's making it with one letter delivery. Maybe I could get a job like that.

A week later Mr. Martino tapped me on the shoulder as I was skinning a rabbit. Nonno would have been proud of me, how neatly I slipped the skin off inside out. I knew what to do with rabbits, but chickens stink. "Peppino, take this package over to Gianni's for Mr. Beretta. He's having a party tomorrow." He stood and watched as I wiped off my hands on my apron, rinsed them in the sink, and threw the apron across the metal stool. He plopped the big paper-wrapped bundle into my arms. "I know it's heavy. Don't drop it. He needs a big roast to make beef sandwiches. Don't take any money. Now go."

He really must like Mr. Beretta, I thought, giving him all this meat. That roast could feed twenty people. I set it back down on the block, put on my jacket, and headed down the street to Gianni's with it. Mr. Salerno was there wiping off tables. "Just go in the back," he said, turning toward the rear door and lifting his chin. "He's with his friends back there." I pushed the door open with my hip so I wouldn't drop the meat. Five men sat around a table playing cards. In the middle there was a pile of chips and money. Mr. Beretta was smoking his cigar just like before.

"*Scusi,*" I said. "I have a package for you from Martino's." The card players stopped and stared at me.

"Just set it down. What's your name, kid?"

"Peppino, I mean Joe."

"Do you talk?"

"Mostly Italian, but I'm learning, sir."

He laughed, not a very nice laugh. The other players snickered. "I mean *silenzio*. Can you keep your mouth shut?" I remembered the men of the *borsa nera* after the war. "I know how to do that," I said. "I learned it in the war."

"You know that cop, McNulty? Big guy, light hair?"

"*Si.*"

"Talk English, kid. He's going to buy some hamburger from Martino this afternoon. I want you to give him this letter. He'll expect you to wait on him. Keep your eyes open." He reached over to his jacket hanging on the back of a chair and opened it. As the lining swung open, there was a loud clunk as his gun hit the chair. He pulled an envelope out of the pocket. "Can you do it? Don't lose it. Here's $10 for you." I held out my hand for it. *"Silenzio, capisce?"* He handed me the letter. He looked straight at me, his dark eyes drilling into me. I wouldn't dare fail.

So now I had a job, a job as good as Dominic's. I wondered if I could hide money in Papá's sofa. The plastic covers were so stiff, but maybe I could tape it under the cushion.

*Chapter 20*
# Meeting Mr. S.

We walked over to Santa Maria Addolorata later in November. The thin wet snow during the night had frozen to a flat sheet of ice on the sidewalk. Mamma walked between Papá and me, holding on to both of us so she wouldn't slip. Her belly was getting big with the American baby now and her coat hardly buttoned. We walked slow. Kids dashed past us on both sides, hoping to get into church and sit down before Sister Salvatora noticed they were late. The bells had almost finished ringing.

Mamma slipped slightly. We caught her. "We should have bought overshoes for you, Lucia. It's so slippery on the street. If you fall it could hurt the baby," Papá said.

"Waste of money," she replied. "I don't walk outside much. We can get them after Christmas when they're on sale. Just hang on to me." We kept going. The owner of Gianni's restaurant was crossing the street just ahead of us, and stepped to the side out of Mamma's way. *"Ciao Signor Salerno,"* I said. I turned to Mamma. "He's got the restaurant—you know where Dom gets the sandwiches to bring to the outfit guys. You know, Dominic's job that he's learning."

He held out his hand to Papá and then to Mamma. Everybody murmured *piacere* and nodded their heads. Mamma hesitated a bit and seemed to be thinking. She looked at him closely. "Is that your restaurant around the corner? Near Martino's butcher shop?" She just stood there talking, so we had to stay.

*"Si,"* he said. "I am the owner. It's a family business. Dominic runs errands for us. My own sons do too, especially Cesare. We call him Cookie. Why do you ask?"

"I worry about Dominic," Papá said. "He tells me he's learning to work for an outfit. He brings home too much money. What is he doing for these people? Nothing he can do is worth $20."

"He just runs errands. You have to understand, *Signora*, this is Chicago. We close our eyes, not see too much, not hear too much. Everyone gets some privacy. It's the Chicago way. Let's go in. Mass will be starting."

Mamma pressed her lips together and narrowed her eyes. As he walked away she hissed at me, "Stay away from them. Chicago way or not, this family is having nothing to do with them, understand?"

I nodded. There goes my chance to make money. I can't let her find out. Those guys have more than enough to spread around. They can be my gold mine.

Dom was working pretty steady for them by this time. He teamed up with Salerno's kid Cookie and they kept busy. They delivered messages. They brought lunches from the restaurant, down the street to the politicians who played poker at the Northwest Civic Committee. They ran out to get them cigarettes. They watched and listened and learned.

I asked Dom one time, "Aren't you afraid you'll get in trouble?"

"Trouble? These guys are big, Peppino. They give the trouble. Even the cops are afraid of them. I watch myself. Mr. Beretta likes me. Says I might get into the outfit later if I play my cards right. Cookie too. We're on his good side."

"I heard there's another gang over by Taylor Street. There was a shootout."

"You heard that? Who'd you hear from? Is this going around the neighborhood?"

"People talk all the time when they're waiting for us to cut their meat," I said. "They don't think we're listening. You'd be surprised what I learn while I'm weighing up lamb chops. Mr. Martino says I have to just hear and say nothing. 'Let it all drop down in your head like a rock in a deep well,' he told me. I know a lot and I think Mamma could be right. She has a good nose for trouble. I like to make money but I don't want to get shot."

"You just have to watch yourself, Peppino. They can't shoot everybody. We got through the war didn't we? There were bombs all over and here we are. Don't be a *vigliacco*, a scaredy-cat. I'm gonna move up in my life. Mr. Beretta says I'm smart and puts his arm around me. He doesn't say that to everybody."

*Chapter 21*
# Christmas with Nicola

Before Christmas one Sunday Mamma seemed different. She kept getting up from the dinner table and walking around, rubbing her back. "What's the matter, Lucia? Do you think it's your time?" Papá said.

"I don't feel too bad. I don't like to go to a hospital. Maria Giuseppe in Italy did a good job bringing babies." She stopped for a minute and seemed to hold her breath. Then she went on. "Get the boys to help you clean up." She walked slowly around the kitchen, holding on to the chairs as she went.

Dom and I pitched in with Papá to clear the table. Papá kept glancing over to watch Mamma. Suddenly she held on to her belly and cried softly. "I think we have to go soon, Gino. The streetcars only run once every half hour. I don't think I can wait more than that."

"Streetcar! We're not going in any streetcar. No matter what it costs, we'll take a cab." She didn't argue, for once. "Peppino, call the telephone. Say your mother is having a baby, send a cab."

I dug into the dish for a nickel, put it in and rattled the hook for the operator. "Send a cab," I said. "Send it quick. 1120 West Grand Avenue. A baby's coming."

Five minutes later a car honked downstairs and Mamma and Papá went slowly down, heading for the hospital. I hoped she'd be safe. In Italy the hospital was where people die. Does the doctor think that she's going to die with this American baby? I kept thinking and worrying until Dom yelled at me. "American babies are born in hospitals, *stupido!* You'll see. She'll be home in a week with the new kid, no worse for the wear. Your mother is tough. You know that. It takes more than a baby to hold her down."

Then I felt better. It was true. She was as tough as weeds. By Christmas we'd all be back to normal.

And we were. The baby boy came home with Mamma a few days later. We called him Nicola after her father and planned the Baptism for the week before Christmas. Mimmo's parents, Mr. and Mrs. DiNardi, were to be godparents. We all had a lot to do, getting pastries ready, making sure our clothes were in good shape for the church. Mamma made

herself a new dress. Her coat fit now, so she didn't
have to make another one. We spread the word
among the *paesani* and close neighbors that coffee
and treats would be served in our apartment after the
church.

It was so cold that day in the church that
there was a skin of ice on the holy water. The priest
wore his coat over his vestments and when the cold
water hit Nicola's head his scream echoed against
the marble walls. Mamma bundled him up right
away in about six blankets and huddled over him.
"*Basta, Padre*, enough Father. He doesn't need
any more prayers. I'm taking him home before he
freezes."

"*Vabbene*, very well. He's God's child now,
and yours to protect. I'll come over later. I haven't
had real *pasta reale* or *taralli* since I came to
Chicago."

Once back home and inside, we warmed up
quickly, getting things set out. And with everyone
wedged into our four small rooms, it got so hot we
had to open a window. The Salerno's came along with
the other neighbors, and Mr. Salerno gave Mamma a
*busta,* an envelope from Mr. Beretta with fifty dollars
in it for a Baptism present. Mamma was shocked
to see almost a week's pay inside, but Mr. Salerno
said, "Mr. Beretta has respect for your son. He likes
to see a smart boy do well." Mamma put it in her
purse.

By Christmas Eve we had put up a Christmas
tree. It was the first one Mamma and I ever saw,
but Papá said everyone needs one. The *Germanesi*

brought them to America and now Americans are supposed to have them. Papá wanted us to be an American family now. We gave presents too, another American custom. Papá gave Mamma a necklace from Goldblatt's, and gave me a new sweater that was "machinery-made." Dominic hauled a heavy package up the stairs with a phonograph in it, and six records. "How could you buy such a fancy thing?" Mamma wanted to know. "It must cost over a hundred dollars."

"It fell off a truck," Dom said. "See, here's a dent. I got it for a bargain."

"As long as you paid for it, Dominic." She raised one eyebrow. "Be a good boy. Keep out of trouble."

*Chapter 22*
# Hard Winter

The excitement wore off as winter went on. Nicola had a set of lungs and didn't mind using them. Mamma walked back and forth with him in the night a lot so the other people in the building wouldn't complain. During the day she was tired and crabby. Because it was so cold, no washing could be hung out on the porch, so we ducked under damp diapers every time we crossed the kitchen. It was too cold to play outside, even if I had the time, but the butcher shop and homework kept me busy.

And there was a lot of cooking to do. Papá, Dominic and I all ate a lot, and most times Uncle Carlo was under foot too. The weather was so cold and snowy that year that all the road construction was stopped, so he had no paycheck. He lived with a group of six men who shared a three-room apartment in shifts. The night workers would sleep in the day, and the day workers could sleep in the same beds at night. It was cheap all right, and they were friends so they usually got along. It was only a problem if one of them overslept, or forgot to wash up, or put his feet in the bed with shoes on. He liked to come to us to have a warm shower. He left his dirty clothes for Mamma too. We had warm water in our building, but she didn't have a washing machine, so she washed it all by hand in the sink and hung it up in the kitchen. A trip to the stove was an obstacle course between damp shirts and diapers. "I left a beautiful home for this," she grumbled. "I wish I'd stayed in Italy."

I tried to help once in a while, carrying my screaming baby brother up and down between the plastic couch and the gas heater. He wasn't much company, and wouldn't be any fun for a long time. But Papá was thrilled with him. Nico just had to gurgle and Papá would glow like he was seeing a miracle. I guess he didn't have any fun with me when I was a baby. Now Nico was his new toy.

Uncle Carlo took a turn walking the baby too."You'd be a good father, *Carluccio*," Mamma said one day. "You have the right touch. Nico likes you better than me."

"I don't know," he said. "I don't want to be tied down to a family. I like to be an uncle. I can come and go."

The best thing in that long winter was the letter. When it came, it was a mess. The thin crinkly paper was all wrinkled up and it looked as if people had stepped on it. The name Binetti had a wrong

address under it. Another Binetti lived over on
Racine Avenue. We didn't know them. They had
scratched it out and put another address which
wasn't ours either. The third try somebody got it
right. It had a lot of Italian stamps canceled in Bari.
Who did we know in Bari? None of our relatives lived
in the city. Mamma wanted to wait until Papá came
home from work but I nagged her until she steamed
it open over the pasta pot.

Inside there was a short note from *Don
Silvestro,* our old priest at home. It was wrapped
around another small letter from Rome. We couldn't
believe our eyes to see Rachel's writing. She wrote
that once she got back to Rome, she had married her
fiancé, Primo, and now they had a new baby boy.
They were working in their bookshop. The Nazis
hadn't burned it down, just trashed it. They repaired
it and had found a lot books hidden in the cellar
and closets, so they had things to sell. They hoped
to move to Israel once the baby could walk. Primo
had a cousin in the publishing business there. They
were saving every penny. They wanted to be part of
a new nation, and were fed up with Rome and Italy
in general. Rachel wanted us to know she would
always remember her time with us, and said she still
has her crooked Hanukkah candles that I found for
her during the war. She wished us all a good life and
happiness. It was a sweet letter, sweet and serious as
she was.

When Papá came home from work we made
him read it out loud to all of us again. "Does this
mean you were concealing a Jewish person from the

Nazis?! Lucia, you are crazy. You could have been shot."

"The Nazis were always on the lookout for Jews, Papá," I told him. "We had a lot of people come into town from other places during the war. They stayed with families. We kids thought they had strange names, Italian names we never heard before. They were really quiet—didn't do *Passeggiata* after dinner, didn't come to church. Others went to church but they kneeled at the wrong times and didn't know the prayers. When they helped out at the farms they didn't know how to prune the trees. They were city people and they acted scared when military was around. Once the Nazis were licked, they all went away. I guess they went home. Rachel worked upstairs, for the mayor."

"Weren't you afraid of the soldiers though, Peppino? How did you manage?"

"I just lied, Papá. It wasn't so hard. I hated them. My heart was pounding under my ribs when I talked to the *Hauptmann* (Nazi Captain). He asked what I knew about 'this person who had to show her papers.' I said I didn't know, she was just a maid. I said I didn't know where she was, and he kept staring down at me through his one-eye eyeglass. I gave the salute and swore that I was loyal to Italy. I was glad the ammo dump blew up just then because he ran out and raced off on his motorcycle."

"The ammo dump blew up? You lied to a *Hauptmann*? A Nazi Captain? How could you have the nerve to do these things? All for the sake of a stranger?"

"She wasn't a stranger. The Germans took her fiancé away. She didn't have a family. Nazis were after her. We had to help her."

Mamma chimed in. "*Sono cristiani,* Gino. Human beings. Nobody should wreck their lives. Driving them like animals into trains. Burning down their shops. The Nazis had no shame, no mercy. We just did what anyone would do. Share food and keep our mouths shut. She taught me a few good recipes. She was good company, almost like an older daughter. I had no one else."

"I never knew what you were going through, Lucia. Never had any idea. I only worried about bombs, not people. I thought you were safe on our land." Papá put his arms around both of us, squishing us together, and a tear rolled down his cheek. He seemed just like Nonno then. "How lucky you were to survive. I wish I could have helped. From now on I'll protect you."

Nico started fussing for Mamma then so Dom and I were left sitting with Papá on the plastic couch. "I've been wanting to talk to you boys alone," he said. "My wife found a roll of twenty-dollar bills in your pants pocket when she did the wash, Dominic. Where did all that money come from?"

"I do errands for people," Dom said.

"And Peppino, Mamma found money under the couch cushion here when she cleaned. It was in an envelope stuck to the bottom. There was $60 there. There's something wrong here. Kids shouldn't have this kind of money to hide. I promised to protect you. I'm afraid I may have to protect you from yourselves."

"It's just extra work, Papá," I said. "You know, the story about the streets of gold. It's not true. All the streets I see are snowy and wet and full of strangers. I want to get that gold."

"I have to tell you boys something. Did you ever hear about the Black Hand?"

"No." We shook our heads.

"In New York there were Italians who'd leave a note on a business: Pay up or else. They'd sign it with a big black handprint. A few days later they would go around to collect. Owners who didn't pay got their stores trashed or burned down. A few were bombed. Everybody was scared and they paid up. The crooks got away and made a nice living."

"But not here, right?"

"We have a few. They're not organized, so it's here and there. An Italian detective called Petrosino got a team together in New York and rounded them up. Later when he visited his hometown in Italy, somebody killed him. Crooks have long memories."

"Why tell us? We're not in New York. We're not putting signs on stores. We just carry messages and do errands. This is different, it's just business."

"I tell you because that's how it starts. Kids see all the money and the fancy suits and big cars and think it's a good deal. Later when they try to back out, they can't. They're in too deep, they know too much. Crooks don't want information passed around."

I remembered what Mr. Beretta said about *silenzio*. I started to open my mouth, but Dom cut me off. "Don't worry, *Signor* Binetti. We'll be careful. I know how to handle myself." Papá patted us on the shoulders and went off toward the kitchen to visit with Mamma and bounce Nico on his lap. "We'll keep low," Dom said. "Just a bit of work here and there. Don't tell your parents anything more. They don't have to know everything you do. After all, your father wrote after the war that you are a man now. Be one."

## Chapter 23
# Caught by the INS

March started out well, with our saint's day,
the feast of *Maria Santissima di Constantinopoli.*
We all marched in the procession behind the
musicians, right in front of the heavy platform
carrying the holy statue. It took eight strong men
to carry it and they swayed as they walked. As we
walked around the neighborhood, people rushed up
to pin money and bits of jewelry to the statue's dress.
Then we went back to the church, put the statue away
and most of the neighborhood went to a big dinner
in a restaurant. It cost eight dollars each, but people
saved up. It was too important to miss. It was just
like being back home, and nobody wanted to miss
it.

There were always the critics, though.
Mimmo's mom, who by now was our *commara* and

demanded respect, said, "You should see what the Sicilians do. They have a really big band, at least fifteen musicians, and they have a wire over the street on a slant. A little girl in an angel costume slides down over the street blessing everyone. And their fireworks are twice as loud." We agreed to go see the Sicilians when their feast, *Lauretana,* came around at the end of summer.

That night around nine, the phone rang. "Telephone," called Mamma, as if we didn't hear it too. Papá went into the hall to answer it.

"It's for you, Lucia. It's your brother. He sounds upset."

Mamma handed Nico to Papá as she went into the hall. We could hear her end of the conversation. "You're where? The police station? *Carluccio! Cos' a fatto?* (What did you do?)" We waited. "You have to stay in jail? It's where?" More waiting. "Peppino, come and write this down for me." I grabbed a sheet out of my notebook and scrabbled around for a pencil. "*Fa fretta, Peppino.* Hurry up!" I did the best I could, writing part in Italian and part in English. It didn't help that Mamma was crying.

The story was that we would have to find a lawyer to get Uncle Carlo out of jail. We didn't know any lawyers. Papá asked around at work next day and a friend told him to ask the precinct captain. Papá took a day off from work and we went to the precinct captain. He walked us over to see the mayor's office, with its beautiful wood paneling and marble floors. We were so impressed that he knew the mayor. Then he gave us the name of his lawyer friend, Mr. Benson.

So then we went to see him. His office was almost
as fancy. I started thinking this is going to cost a lot
of money. I helped Papá translate. Back and forth
the bargaining went, Mamma and Papá discussed in
Italian what we could afford and then I told it to the
lawyer. The price kept adding up and I wondered if
Uncle Carlo was worth it. Three hundred dollars, up
front. Six weeks of Papá's pay would really hurt us,
but we finally agreed.

Mamma and I went to get him. We walked
with Officer Morici down the long hallway between
the cells. Prisoners shouted out and clanged their
metal cups on the bars and whistled. "Pay no mind
to them," Officer Morici said. "They're not worthy of
your notice."

"Hey kid, aren't you kind of young to be
in here?" one hollered. I made my face hard and
ignored him.

A voice close beside me jeered, "What a
crybaby, hiding behind his ma! Hey, cutie pie—need
a new dad for that kid?"

"*Va fa' 'n culo!*" I hissed. "Up yours!" I stuck
my finger up in front of his face, but on my side
of the bars. "*Tu sei fesso!*" The prisoner looked
surprised.

Mamma jerked me by the elbow. "*Zito.* Quiet.
These are *ladri, assassini, non si scherzan'*, don't
play around."

Officer Morici hid a smile behind his
mustache. "It's safe enough now when the bars are
closed," he remarked. "You probably don't want them
to get a good look at you though. They remember

faces and they won't be in here forever."

So Uncle Carlo was released. They told him he had 90 days before he had to go back to Italy. He said he'd pay Mamma back. She said he'd better find a wife so he could stay. He said he'd think about it. He went back to his empty apartment. All his roommates had cleared out and gone into hiding once the Immigration Service showed up.

Life went back to normal. After a few days Uncle Carlo told us what happened. He had been helping a neighbor bottle his homemade wine and a man in their building reported that they were making more than 100 gallons. A hundred gallons was legal on the permit, as long as you kept it in the family. They had made 200. Cops came, asked for papers and of course Uncle Carlo didn't have any. He was a poor liar too and that did it for him. He landed in jail. And now we were out $300.00.

Dominic was very quiet whenever we talked about Uncle Carlo's jail problem. After a few days I asked him, "Still working for Mr. Beretta?"

"Yeah. I'm gonna need help later this week, too. Cookie got his tonsils out and I have heavy stuff to deliver. Wanna help? Just delivery. Late, maybe around 11:30. Probably we'll do the drop Wednesday." I helped, got my $20, snuck back into our house and no one was the wiser. We did it three weeks in a row and then Cookie's tonsils got better.

Then on a job with Cookie, Dom got picked up and we got another call from the jail. It meant another trip, this time to the part where they have the tough kids. Papá was working, so I told Mamma I would explain to the judge that Dom was a very good hard-working kid who survived a war. As soon as we sat down in the courtroom, I jumped up,waving my hand. "Let me explain, Judge," I cried. "I can tell you about Dominic."

"Are you representing Dominic Capresi here, the defendant?" the judge asked me. "Are you his lawyer?"

"No, Judge, just his friend. He can't afford a lawyer."

"The court will appoint him one, then. You are not qualified to speak for him."

"But that will take a long time and he needs to come home with us. He doesn't have any family here."

"Very well, I suppose a friend can speak for him if he consents. Dominic, do you consent to have your friend here—what's your name again?—speak for you?" Dom nodded.

"I'm Peppino, I mean Giuseppe Binetti. He's been my friend since I was a child."

"You're how old now, Mr. Binetti?"

"Fourteen."

"I see. What can you tell me about the character of Dominic Capresi? That will help me make a fair decision."

"He's smart. He helps his friends when things are tough. In Italy during the war when there wasn't anything to eat, he could always find a couple eggs or bread somewhere and share it. One time we stole two chickens right out from the Nazis' noses. He knows how to hold their beaks to keep them quiet."

"You're telling me he's a skillful thief?"

"He only steals from bad people, Judge. We were hungry."

The judge shuffled through his papers, found one, pushed his glasses up on his nose and read it. "Now to the matter at hand. The charge is that Dominic Capresi was apprehended loading up his pockets with expensive items in Marshall Field's store, things he couldn't use himself, such as nylon stockings and scarves. How do you explain that?"

"He probably wanted to help some poor ladies," I explained. "Dominic is very kind that way and he owes a lot of favors to people who invite him for dinners."

"It's stealing just the same. We are not Nazis and the war is over. We have to pay for what we want. If he's hungry he can go to Chicago Commons and get free soup and sandwiches. He has no excuse to steal."

"If he promises to be honest and obey my parents, Judge, will you let him come home with us? My mother will make him behave himself."

The judge turned to Mamma. "Do you agree to this, madam? Will you be responsible for this boy?" I translated for Mamma and she nodded solemnly to the judge. "*Si, d'accordo, Signore Giudice,*" she said. "I agree, Judge."

"Done," said the judge and rapped with his gavel. "Pay $25 court costs to the clerk as you exit." He turned back to Dominic. "I don't expect to see you back here again Mr. Capresi. If you're arrested again you'll go to my colleague on the third floor who deals with criminals. Be careful." Luckily the judge didn't ask him for any papers.

Dom came back home with us seeming very cheerful. "See, Peppino, it's a sign. I'm going to be big some day. I just have to move up a step at a time in the outfit. It beats cleaning chickens. You did pretty good in there. Maybe you should be a lawyer instead of a butcher."

Dom kept working with Cookie, though. He'd sneak out after we went to bed. He had copied the key for the door downstairs and he knew where to put his feet on the steps so they wouldn't squeak. He'd tell me about it on the side when Mamma was too busy with the baby to hear. Most of the night work was unpacking trucks and putting the things in a warehouse. During the day they ran errands. He was surprised that there was often a whole truckload of things for homes, like radios and phonographs, fancy lamps, rugs, refrigerators, all kinds of stuff. "I never thought I'd be a furniture mover," he laughed. "I wish they'd move their stuff when it's light, though. It's hard to carry in the dark without tripping and the driver is always telling us to keep quiet." I sneaked a peek in the pocket of his pants that were dumped on the chair as he slept. His roll of cash was getting bigger all the time.

**Chapter 24**

# Payoff from the Outfit

I started dreaming of money. I dreamt that
I was on a boat and it landed on an island where
there were piles of gold. I dreamt I found a winepress
standing on the street and it was filled with ten-dollar
bills. I dreamt that a lady with a sword saw me taking
the money and came after me. That time I woke up
yelling for help and Dom had to put his hand over
my mouth. But money was on my mind: too much in
Dom's pocket and not enough in Mamma's purse.
With so many to feed and only Papá's paycheck,
we were eating beans a lot, like we did in the war.
*Pasta e faggiole, ceci e pasta, cannellini* soup. If
you could make it out of dried beans and pasta, that
was what we ate. How is this better than the war, I
wondered. We still have mean people controlling the

neighborhood, we're still short of money, and we're still eating beans and saving every penny. On top of it we had more people to take care of. Nico was a cute baby, as babies go, but he was a lot of work and Mamma had no time for me any more.

"I'm tired of beans and pasta," I complained to Mamma one day. "If I see another bean I'm going to throw up."

"You always say that about beans. You're lucky to have them. Do you think you're *u' barone,* a baron? Your father works hard to feed us. It isn't his fault there's no room for a garden here."

"OK, Mamma, OK. Maybe I can get a few pork neckbones from Martino on Saturday for gravy."

"That's better. Work and get something for us. Don't stand around complaining."

Nico let out a yell that rattled the cups on the shelf. We should get him opera lessons, I thought. "Go get your brother and keep him quiet while I finish cooking," Mamma said.

"But I have homework."

"Your father will be home soon. Homework can wait." I got the little crybaby out of his crib and carried him around and around the apartment. I was wearing a track in the floor. Even living in the same house, I missed Mamma. She didn't watch over my homework any more and we hardly talked. She didn't understand what I was doing in school and didn't have time. Nico and Papá used her up. I began to think Dom had the right idea. I should just grow up and make my own way.

"We need a third guy," Dom told me a week later.

"No stealing," I told him. "Mamma would kill me."

"It's not really stealing, Peppino. The restaurant owner owes money to Mr. Beretta He wants us to go get it."

"What do I have to do?"

"You just have to stand outside and watch for the cops. If you spot one, give us the signal and we'll come out."

"Why do we care about cops? And who's 'we'?"

"Me and Cookie. He just scares the owner a little, we get the money and we run out. Deliver it to Mr. Beretta tomorrow. All you have to do is be the guard."

That didn't sound so bad. Not exactly stealing. I could just stand outside, watch and get paid for it. I could do that.

That night I went to bed on time. I heard Mamma in the rocking chair sing *Ninna, nanna* over and over to Nico until he fell asleep. Papá and Mamma went to bed too. I heard the bed squeak as they got in and then at last Papá's snoring. I heard the downstairs lady's clock chime eleven, and finally it was quiet. I crept out of bed. Out of the window I saw Dom already down in the back, blending into the shadows. I slipped on my jacket, tiptoed to the door holding my shoes and quietly opened it. I slipped a card in to hold the lock open. A few careful steps and I was down and out for my first job.

Dom pulled a gun out of his pocket. "Cookie got me this."

"A gun? You're crazy, Dom."

"It's just for show. Cookie says I need it so they know I'm serious." Just then Cookie showed up. We stopped talking.

"C'mon. Let's move," he said. "We got a job to do." He started walking fast and we had to keep pace with him.

When we got to the restaurant, the owner was just locking up. Cookie walked in and talked to him. The guy started shaking. I couldn't see why. Then I saw Cookie had a knife out and was holding it close to his ear. Then a flash of the knife. The owner raised his arm to push Cookie away, and the knife sliced into his arm. Dom shot at the window as Cookie grabbed money out of the cash register. Out of the corner of my eye I saw two cops walking our way. At the sound of the breaking glass they started to run towards us. The fatter one rushed into the restaurant. The taller one called, "I'll get the kids, Ralph. Get help for the man on the ground."

"Go, go!" Dom shouted as he ran past me. Cookie took off in the other direction with the money. We ducked into an alley. Dom dropped the gun and it went off, bullets hitting the brick wall and bouncing. We dived behind a big garbage bin. The cop fired and I felt a hard, burning pain go through my leg.

The cop stopped and looked, putting his gun away. "Lousy Dago kids," he said. "They're ruining the neighborhood." He turned back toward the restaurant.

As I rolled over to get up from behind the bin, my leg hurt bad. When I tried to stand up, my leg folded. The pain washed over me. "I'm hit,

Dom," I told him, trying hard not to cry. *Dio mio* it hurt.

"Help! Help!" Dom shouted.

"The cops? You're calling the cops? Are you crazy?" I hissed, gasping for breath and holding my hurt leg.

As the policeman turned back, running to see what happened, Dom kicked his gun behind the trash can. " My friend is shot. He can't stand up."

The policeman knelt beside me. He looked to see that I was breathing and then looked down at my pants leg where the blood was soaking through. "You're hit all right," he said.

"It hurts so bad," I sobbed.

"You're pumping a lot of blood. Don't try to move." He pulled out his small radio and talked into it. "I'm getting an ambulance. Here," he said to Dom. He took Dom's hand and pushed it down tight at the top of my leg. "Hold tight right here. Press with all your might. Here at the top of his leg where the big artery goes through. Don't let go."

We waited there for what seemed like hours. Maybe it was really fifteen minutes. The other cop came over from the restaurant to see what happened. "The other kid got away with the money," he said. "The owner just has a cut. I patched him up with band-aids. What's the deal here?"

"Kid got shot through the thigh. The ambulance is on the way. I only fired at the trash can to scare them. It was an accident."

The siren stopped as the ambulance pulled up. The attendants lifted me quickly to a stretcher and then into the ambulance. Dom and the cop climbed in, the siren wailed again and we drove straight to County Hospital. A nurse came to the door, took one look, and waved the attendants inside. We rolled into a big room. People were lined up in chairs and on rolling carts. Kids were crying. Everybody looked worried.

"Gunshot, room 3," she called as we rolled past them into a little room.

After a few minutes a tired young doctor came in. "Don't you kids ever learn?" he said wearily. "This is the fourth gunshot I have tonight and it's only midnight. What were you doing?"

"Injured in the course of a robbery," the cop said. "Running from the scene."

"Collecting a debt," Dom mumbled.

"That's what you call it? Now your friend is hurt bad." Dom hung his head.

" We need to contact your parents before surgery. Where do you live? Don't let go of his leg! Just talk."

Dom gave him a false address, 1882 East Ohio. It wasn't a good one, though. It would have been in the lake. The doctor looked disgusted. "Don't even know the city and you're already in trouble."

"Tell the truth, kids," the cop said. "The doc just said 'surgery' and that's serious. He'll have to get the bullet out and stop the bleeding. Do you have a phone number and an address?"

I gave her our real address and the phone number. When the cop heard 1120 West Grand Avenue, he looked up. "The Grand Avenue mob

works around that neighborhood," he said. "You kids
don't know any of them do you? There's a Sammy
and the *capo* is Mr. Beretta If you meet any of them
stay away. They have a regular business going there,
stealing truckloads of things and reselling."

"We go to school, Officer," Dom said quickly.
"And Peppino, I mean Joe here, works at a butcher
shop."

"Best to get off the streets earlier, though.
This accident wouldn't have happened if you were
home in bed. You could have been hurt by that young
hoodlum that held up the restaurant."

I started to pass out as the nurse went out to
the desk to call. The doctor took a big scissors and
sliced my pants all the way through. Dom had to take
his hands up to get out of the way of the cutting, and
I could see blood starting to pump out again. "You're
losing a lot of blood," the doctor said. He called out
to the nurse, "I need an IV setup in here, two liters
of saline and cross-match for blood." He gave me a
shot and that's the last I remember until I woke up in
recovery room.

I hurt everywhere. My arm was laid out flat,
taped to a flat board and there were needles in it
attached to tubes from bottles of blood and clear
liquid hanging from a frame. My leg was wrapped in
bandages. I felt woozy when I tried to lift my head.
My clothes were gone and I had a sort of shirt on
under the covers. A nurse came over and looked at
my eyes. "Welcome back to the world," she said.
"Your operation is done. They got the bullet out and
stopped the bleeding. They fixed your artery and

stitched up the tear in the muscles. You're lucky they got you here when they did. You had lost a lot of blood. If you have to throw up, use this little pan." She tucked a small pan under my chin. "Let me know if the pain is too much. I can give you another shot." Off she went.

I heard someone crying off the side and turned my head a bit. It was Mamma. Papá was holding on to her and crying too. "I was a fool to bring you to America," he murmured. "At least you were safe in our town after the war. We knew what we had, knew where the dangers were."

I kept my eyes closed. Papá wouldn't want me to see him cry.

"Don't blame yourself, Gino," Mamma whispered, patting him on his head like a child. "You wanted to do a good thing."

"And now Dominic might be arrested. We'll have to help him. We owe his parents to stand by him, right or wrong." I had never heard Papá mourn like this. He was always so quiet and sturdy, a man you could lean on and trust.

"I'll write and explain to his mother," Mamma said. "Catarina was always my friend, even if her husband was trouble. She knows Dominic is just like his father, a box of fireworks ready to go off. Maybe we can steer him to a better kind of life."

They looked over at me then to see if I was still asleep. I opened my eyes, blinking like I just woke up. They sniffed and shook themselves, wiping their eyes and hoping I didn't see. "We were worried," Mamma said.

Papá nodded, his deep brown eyes ringed with

red. "The doctor says you'll be all right. A little limp
is nothing. Even Nonno limps, remember?"

"Will I lose my leg?" I asked them.

"The doctor says no. They saved your leg."

"Can I walk?"

"In a couple of weeks."

Just then two orderlies came in. They gently
moved me over to a rolling cart. They took me down
the hall to a regular room with four beds, one of them
empty. That bed was for me. They lifted me onto it,
adjusted my arm board, and put the basin under my
chin. "You'll be in this ward, 307-3, for a few days,"
they said. They pinned a plastic push-button to the
sheet near my empty hand. "If you need anything,
like a drink of water or a bedpan, push this button.
Somebody will come to help."

Mamma and Papá found empty chairs and
dragged them near my bed. Soon Dom came in and
pulled a chair over too. Mamma gave him a look that
would have killed a dragon. "You see what your little
adventure has done to my son? He's your friend. Now
he suffers."

Papá nodded. "You've disgraced us and your
own family. How can you face yourself?" And then
it all came out, every nasty word of it. Dom spilled
the whole story. He said I was just a watcher. That
Cookie was the scary one, and that Cookie took off
with the money. He didn't mention the gun.

Mamma didn't miss a word, even if it was
in English. "Don't blame Cookie, Dominic. Blame
yourselves. There's no such thing as easy money. This
'work' as you call it is a good way to get your picture

up on a stone in the cemetery."

"Police don't shoot by accident," Papá said, glaring at him. "What were you doing out so late? Why did you bring my son into it?"

Then Mamma turned on me. "Why are you spending time with that Cookie—a stupid name for a stupid boy— when you know he works for the people in Salerno's back room? Why did you sneak out with Dominic in the night to do this job? Your job is at the butcher shop." She had a list of questions that would make a lawyer cry for mercy. "And now we have a hospital bill. How can we pay?" Nobody wanted to give the answers. There were no good ones.

I started to throw up and Papá found the small basin and held it for me. I had never seen his face so sad. He started to talk quietly, but his serious voice got our attention more than shouting. "I've lived here in Chicago for more than twenty years. I came to work here when I was younger than you, Dominic. I faced the same problems you face, but I didn't have a house or a mother or father to help me. I got a job digging to build the sewer lines. Then I lived with friends until I could save up enough for a room of my own. I saw gangsters making suitcases full of money selling liquor when it was against the law. I also saw the bodies of their enemies fished out of the Chicago River. When you work for those people you take your life in your hands and nobody is crazy or foolish enough to confront them. The only way is to keep your head down and stay out of their path. Bow and disappear. Our families did that for hundreds of years in Italy when enemies overran us."

When he stopped for breath, Mamma took over. "I could report you to Immigration, you know, Dominic," she said. "You'd have to go home and face your father. You sneaked into this country. You can sneak out again. I'm writing to your mother tomorrow. She knows you're with us."

"Please, *per pietá*, have pity," Dom pleaded. He had good reason, knowing his father's temper. Everyone in our little town except my mother was afraid of Dom's father. There was no way he could go back to Bitritto without his father finding out. "I'll do anything. I don't want to be sent back."

"You will need to have a penance. Don't look at me with big sad eyes, Dominic. You were acting like a criminal and pulling my boy in with you. For the next month you will be washing all the diapers and hanging them out to dry on the roof. Anyone who wants to look will see what brave gangster boys are good for. You can start the first batch tomorrow morning, before we go to Mass."

"Sister says we're not to work on Sunday," I protested.

"That's a woman's job," stammered Dom. "I'll look stupid."

"As you are, Dominic. As you are. Bringing disgrace to the family. Helping thieves. Getting soiled diaper stains on your fingers is nothing compared to that. You're lucky to be dealing with me and not your father. He'd beat you bloody."

Papá put his hand on Dom's shoulder and stared into his eyes. "You have to get away from those people. Swear to me that you won't go back there."

"But I have a job," Dom started to say. "They depend..."

"Not any more. You're in my hands now," Mamma said, "and I am going to straighten you out, put you in order." She said all this in Italian and it sounded like she was planning to do spring cleaning on Dom. It sounded uncomfortable.

I remembered Mimmo's mother coming to America to straighten out her husband. Maybe that was what women did in America. It was the right kind of job for Mamma. Now Mimmo's parents were Nico's godparents and Mr. DiNardi had a job, came home to his family every night, and gave his paycheck to his wife. I think he was straightened. It might work on Dominic. I knew we were in for it.

## Chapter 25
# Mamma Makes Plans

After I came home on crutches, Mamma made her move. She dropped Nico off with his *commara*, Mrs. DiNardi, and walked me and Dom to Santa Maria school. She marched us past the kids waiting in line for the bell. Kids poked each other and turned to stare at me on my crutches. I stared right back. We went down that same shiny, banana-and-disinfectant-smelling hallway to Sister Vittoria's office. The door was open and Sister was just putting her record of marching music on the turntable. "How can I help you?" she said. "Just give me a minute here." She looked at Mamma again and remembered that we were new. *"Un momento, per favore."* She pointed to a chair near her desk, turned on the phonograph and the sound of a marching band filled the school and spilled out onto the playground. We heard the shuffle of hundreds of feet coming down the hall and up the stairs. She closed her door and sat, pulling her chair up to her desk. She took a record book out of her top drawer and opened it to a list headed 'New Students.' "I think I remember you. Aren't you Peppino Binetti? Now called Joe? You came in the middle of the year, I think. I placed you in the beginners' English class?"

"Last year, Sister. Now eighth grade. Room 12."

"I heard you injured your leg and missed a week of classes. How are you doing now?"

"OK, I guess," I mumbled. "It's still sore."

"How time passes." Her finger traced down, onto another page. "Ah, here I find you. Your grades are fair. You passed everything last year. What do you need from me? Your teacher will give you your make-up work."

Mamma started. "*Una problema difficile. Eppure delicata.*" Mamma edged forward on her chair.

"I can help talk," I said. "Mamma doesn't talk American yet. She goes to lessons but the baby makes it hard to study." I looked over at Mamma and she nodded.

"Just tell her the whole story in English," she told me in Italian. "You know it as well as I do. You can explain what she suggests."

So I told the whole story to Sister Vittoria. Dom kept his head down the whole time. I left out most of what I had done; she didn't need to know everything. When we came to the part about getting shot, Sister gasped and started to say something. Then she stopped herself and said, "Go on."

Finally I came to the point. What could we do to get Dominic out of trouble and keep him out? Sister rummaged in her desk drawer, came up with a well-worn business card, and copied out the information on a small sheet of paper. "You need to see Dan Brindisi. He runs activities for older children and teenagers. He speaks Italian and knows everybody worth knowing. He can point you to work and school for Dominic. He may know how to keep Dominic from being deported as well. He probably knows a good lawyer."

"We already know one for my Uncle," I started to say. Mamma poked me with her elbow. She knew more English than she let on, I guess. She didn't want our business known, even by Sister Vittoria. Mamma leaned over and whispered that I needed the day off to help her. I translated that and Sister Vittoria gave me a hall pass. She wished us good luck.

Out we went into the May sunshine. The warm wind carried the perfume of the bridal wreath and snowball bushes at the end of the school. Flowers always smell better when you're playing hooky. A whole day free from school and free from work! I hoped Dom would leave me out of the story. I felt like flying but the crutches held me back.

We found Mr. Brindisi sorting and stacking gym equipment at his place. The warm wind there smelled more like sweaty gym socks. He scooped up a stray basketball and threw it into a bin as we walked to his office. We went through our routine again. Mamma coached me in Italian, I talked English and

Dom just stood there embarrassed.

"You've got a mess here, Dominic," Brindisi
said. Dom's head snapped up, alert. Now finally
somebody was talking to him. We all listened and
I explained to Mamma as we went. "If the police
decide to press charges, you're going to the criminal
division. Maybe you'll be lucky though. It sounds as
if the cop thinks he shot you by accident and doesn't
want to make a fuss. They already have Cookie on
their watch list. They probably have his fingerprints
all over the restaurant.

"Here's what you have to do," Brindisi
continued. "First, you have to break away from the
gangsters. That's never easy, but it seems like you're
not in too deep yet. People who get close can pay with
their life if they leave. So just don't go on any more of
those trips. Make an excuse. Blame Peppino's mother
here." He grinned at Mamma. She didn't get it.

"Second, you need somebody to sponsor you
so you can stay in America. It can't be Peppino's
family. They have enough to do. I'll help you find
somebody who'll sponsor you and give you a place
to live. You'll have to pay them, it's only right. You
can get a weekend job and give them your paycheck.
I think I know people who'll do it, but you'll have to
stay clean, or the deal will be off.

"Last, you need an education. I can see you're
smart. You have quick wits. You want to get ahead. I
like that. Wells High School has classes that prepare
boys for jobs. You could be an electrician, a plumber,
a carpenter."

Dom looked at him eagerly. "Will they show

me how to fix cars?"

"They do have an auto shop program.
You have to show them you're serious and study
English and math too but it's free except for
textbooks."

I couldn't believe that would be free. The
American soldiers at the end of the war said that, but
I thought they were making it up.

Brindisi wrote down the addresses and phone
numbers we'd need. He said he'd fill out the papers
for us so that Dom could be sponsored. He said we
didn't need a lawyer yet and if we did he'd find us a
cheap one. We only had to fill out a form with all our
names and addresses for his file, and then we were
out in the sunshine again, feeling good. By the end
of the week Dom could be signed up and sponsored
and safe. And I'd get another free day to help make it
happen.

Once Dominic was organized, Mamma and
Papá started planning my life. They wanted to keep
me away from the outfit guys but they still needed
me to make some money. Prices were going up after
the war. Now we had another mouth to feed and he
needed lots of feeding. It wasn't only feeding. Nico
was growing fast and Mamma had to keep up with
the *paesani*. Nico had to look sharp, make *la bella
figura*. His little suits needed to be pressed and
his little white shoes polished. He needed a proper
baby buggy and a special chair at the table. Mamma
wasn't going to let him grow up like me, playing in
the dirt in the garden. The American baby should get
only the best. So I was the natural person to turn to

for another paycheck. I overheard them one day. "Maybe you should take Peppino back home," Papá said. "We still own the house. You can make enough off the farm to live, like you did before. Peppino will be away from the gangs. It breaks my heart to lose you again, but he can be killed here."

"Break the family again? And what about Nico. He's an American."

"Better alive in Italy than dead in America. I can try to get work there in our home town. With the war over, there may be something. We'll just have to make the best of it. I'm so sorry I made you come here, just to have a tragedy like this."

"Move again? We're not *zingari* (gypsies)! And there are no jobs in Italy now. The country is in ruins."

"We have to do what we have to do, Lucia. Peppino could have been killed."

"If we can keep him safe until he gets a job, maybe we can stay. At least he's safe from the gangs with his crutches. They don't want to hire cripples." She started to cry when she said cripples.

"His leg will heal. The butcher shop is a good place to work," Papá said. "He'll never go hungry. Maybe Martino would take him as an apprentice."

"Peppino is too smart," Mamma replied. "He should use his clever mind to make money.

"But, Lucia, my friends at the candy factory say it's a great opportunity to get into the butchers' union. He'll get as big a paycheck as mine in a couple of years."

"Paychecks aren't everything. He also needs more school so he can talk for us. Remember when we had to talk to the lawyer? We need a smart talker in the family. If only he didn't limp. It makes him look weak and who wants a weak lawyer?" She sniffed and rubbed her eyes. "Maybe a good school would put him on the right track."

Papá had a friend in the Italian club where he went every Sunday after dinner. He asked him to let his daughter Ninella teach me more English. I had to go to their house on Wednesday and Friday after school. We sat in the kitchen and she taught me how to say useful things, while her mother cooked. A couple of times she caught me moving over to sit closer to Ninella. "Eyes on your studies, *guaglione!*" she said. "You're here to learn. Marriage comes later."

"Marriage? Who said anything about marriage? Ninella just smells so good," I said. That was a mistake.

"If you come into this house, you must respect my daughter's honor," she said sharply. "My daughter is not a piece of pastry. Otherwise find someone else to teach you. We can get along without that dollar you give me. And your mother is my close friend."

In our neighborhood everybody knew each other, and they all watched out their windows. Now most of them had telephones too, so the mothers knew who was where and what we were doing. A kid couldn't blow his nose without his family knowing about it.

*Chapter 26*
# Uncle Carlo's Decision

A letter arrived with Uncle Carlo's name on it. When he came over for supper Mamma met him at the door with it, wiping her hands on her apron. "It looks official, *Carluccio*. Looks like something from *u'govern'*. Are you in trouble again?"

"Who knows? Governments are crazy. Maybe Peppino can understand it." He slid his finger inside the edge and tore it open. He handed it to me with the letter still inside. It looked official, all typed with the label on the top: United States Immigration and Naturalization Service.

I read it out loud. "Pursuant to our previous correspondence, and in compliance with Public Law Number..."

"Just explain," Mamma said. "We don't know those words anyway."

I went back to reading silently. My eye caught on the phrase "ninety (90) days from" and then I remembered. The court had told Uncle Carlo he had ninety days to find a way to stay in America. Otherwise he had to ship out. That was back in March. The days must be coming to an end. "You have to go back home soon," I told him. "Remember, they told you to get a plan or go back to Italy in 90 days. The days are almost up. When did they catch you?"

Mamma and Uncle Carlo puckered up their eyebrows and started trying to count back. "It was before Dominic got in trouble."

"*Si.*"

"I think it was cold. Were you working then?"

"Oh, now I remember. I was helping bottle Perino's wine. The man in the apartment downstairs reported us, and the cops took everybody off to jail. We weren't doing anything bad."

"You broke a rule," I said. "They pay a lot of attention to rules in America."

"For some," Mamma said. "Look at the people Dom worked for. They break three rules every day before breakfast and they still command the neighborhood."

"*Hai ragione,* Lucia. You're right. But they got us anyway. I think I phoned you from the police station."

"That's it. We just came home from the *Festa* and the phone rang. Now I remember. We'll just have to make a plan, and fast. I'll call my friends and see if they know any nice girl for you to marry, one with citizenship."

"I can't marry an American," Carlo protested. "We could hardly talk to each other."

"I know what I'm doing. I'll find you someone from an Italian family. It will be just like living at home, but better. You'll have company."

"I don't know Lucia. I like it quiet, so I can think. And I don't like to be managed."

"Then you'll have to go back to our mother and the farm. Just let me try. Today is Wednesday. Plan to come over Saturday afternoon for a sandwich. I'll have company then." So Carlo gave in to Mamma, as we all do, and agreed to come on Saturday.

Mamma went to the pastor and asked him if he knew any nice single women with citizenship. A widow would be OK, she thought. By Saturday she had found a few with potential. There was a widow with three small kids a few blocks north. A young lady from Sicily whose fiancé had run off. A cousin of the lady who worked in the grocery store. One by one they came for cookies and coffee, and one by one they left, with only the snack to show for their visit.

I was surprised to see what fancy taste Uncle Carlo had in ladies. One was too tall, one wasn't very pretty, and three kids were more than he could face. He was very picky for a guy who always needed to shave and smelled like a barn even in the city. Time was running out when finally our pastor found the perfect person: single, pretty and born in Capurso, near our hometown. And her citizenship papers came through last year.

Sofia came over on a Sunday afternoon.

Mamma put out her best little cups, a plate of *biscotti* and a big dish of red jello. "How nice of you to come, Sofia," she said. "Have a seat. This is my brother Carlo."

"*Piacere*," Sofia said, and sat.

"You are from Capurso?" Uncle Carlo said politely, dunking his *biscotto* and trying not to get any more spots on his tie.

"*Si.*" The room stayed quiet.

"Tell us about your family," Mamma offered. "We would like to know you better. You said you live alone. How can that be?"

"My parents are decent people. Yet they allowed me to come here alone. They trust me to manage myself. They suffered during the war and want me to find a better life."

"I quit the army and walked home from Sicily after Mussolini was deposed," volunteered Carlo. "Who didn't suffer? You're not telling me anything new."

"Do you have a house?" Sofia asked.

"Never needed one. I stay with friends."

"Do you want a family?"

"Maybe. Families can be difficult."

"Have some more coffee," Mamma said to loosen them up. "The coffee is real now, you know— not *orzo* like we had during the war. The *biscotti* have butter in them too. Eat up."

"I think I would need to have a house if I were to have a family," Sofia commented. "A house makes a person feel complete. Unfortunately I don't have any dowry..."

Uncle Carlo stood up. "I don't want to hurry you, but I've promised my friends a *bocce* game at four."

"I won't hold you, then," Sofia remarked. "Thank you for the hospitality, Signora Binetti. Perhaps we'll meet again." She picked up her purse, pulled on her gloves, straightened the veil on her hat, and headed for the door.

Once she was gone, Mamma exploded. "What are you thinking of, Carlo? She's a nice girl, from our province—a lady, even too good for you."

"You don't see, Lucia. You try too hard. I just couldn't face living with her, working to make sure she has her house and everything she wants, while she looks down her little nose at me when I come home dirty from working on the streets. Nobody is going to make this decision for me. I won't marry someone just to stay here. I'd rather be dead. There's a saying and you know it. *Meglio solo che mal'accompagnato!* (Better alone than in bad company.) I'm going back home. Forget about *l'America*! I know my own land and I'll take care of our mother." He grabbed his hat, plopped it down on his head and walked out, slamming the door behind him.

Mamma put her hand up to her mouth and bit down on the side of her finger. *Che fesso,*" she said. "What a fool!"

**Chapter 27**
# Aiming High

Once the INS sent Uncle Carlo back to Italy, I started getting worried that Mamma would take me back there too. I hardly saw Dom any more now that he was living with the family who had the auto repair shop. He traded his help there for the meals they gave him. They signed him up for a summer class in the evenings at Wells High School so he could learn more English. The teacher told him the men at the Northwest Civic Committee were poor examples. I think she meant their English, but maybe she knew more than we did.

A few times he asked me to help with jobs but I told him my leg still hurt and I'd only slow him down. "You're never going to amount to anything," he told me one day. "The sore leg is just an excuse to stay safe at home like a baby. Together we can really move up in the outfit. Make some real money. Gain some real respect."

"It's a lousy life," I argued back. "You have to sneak around at night. People shoot at you. You have to lie all the time and watch over your shoulder for cops. Besides my family could get hurt."

"Well, that's your decision. After all these years of friendship I thought I could depend on you."

"Depend if you need help," I said, "but don't depend on me for any dirty work. I have other plans."

"Yeah, right. Big plans. I bet I'll have a big car before you. I'll wave as I pass by. Maybe I'll drop in and buy a chicken to help you out."

"I can take care of myself, Dom. You don't have to do me any favors." I headed toward home with a heavy heart.

Papá asked Mr. Martino to take me on as an apprentice butcher and he agreed. That was Mamma's idea. The prospect of a paying job in three years finally won her approval. As soon as school finished I started going to the butcher shop every morning at 6 a.m. to get lessons, and then working the rest of the day for helper pay. Chicago was warming up in June. The fan in the ceiling didn't help cool the shop much. The only good place was the cooler, but my job was out back cleaning the chickens. But a paycheck is a paycheck.

With Dom working on cars and Vito and Carmi busy with odd jobs, my future seemed to be more hard, dirty work. Mamma had cancelled the lessons with Ninella, saying they were a distraction. I asked our priest at the church if he knew a way to get a better job. "Education is the key to success here," he said. "You have to learn all you can and then work like crazy. Work by itself just gives you more work. Americans say you have to 'work smart'."

"I can go to Wells with my friend Dominic," I said. "We could fix cars together."

"Fixing cars is good. Owning the business is better," he said. "Your parents own a bit of land in Italy, right?"

"Yes."

"Wasn't that better than working on somebody else's farm?"

"Of course. We still worked all the time, though."

"Think about this, Peppino. Nobody can take away what you have stored in your mind. Everybody has to work, but what you understand helps you do it well. It gives you choices. Where are the boys in your class going?"

"All public except Herman Schroeder. He's going to St. Ignatius because his dad wants him to be a lawyer."

"Is he smarter than you?"

"His English is better. I don't think he knows more. His life is pretty soft, I think."

"Then why don't you sign up for St. Ignatius? Aim high, Peppino."

So I did, but I didn't tell Mamma. I wrote a letter to St. Ignatius and asked to enroll. A week later I got a letter back. Mamma handed it to me as I came in from work.

"You're getting school letters now? You never

mentioned this to me. We agreed that you would become a butcher."

"I needed to find out, Mamma. Let me read it." It said that I had missed the deadline to apply, that I needed all my grades sent over from Santa Maria, and that I had to take another test, which was given three weeks ago in May. My heart sank. Another year of cutting meat before even taking a test. I could get old this way. "I have to go talk to them, Mamma," I said. "I'll take off tomorrow and go there and talk."

"You have a job to do."

"Mr. Martino will understand. Tuesday is slow anyway. If I can go to a good school, maybe I can become a businessman or a lawyer. Even a doctor. I'm good at taking animals apart at the butcher shop. People's insides can't be so different. And I can make you proud."

Mamma seemed to be thinking that over. "It takes years," she said.

"That's why I have to go tomorrow. I'll get a start."

The next day I dressed up in my best homemade suit and took two buses to St. Ignatius. I sat outside until they opened, then looked for the president's office. I walked around the empty halls, stepping over drop cloths and around piled-up desks until I found it. The secretary said I should see the registrar, but I convinced her it was an emergency. She was surprised that there were school emergencies in June when no one was there but the painters.

Finally a priest came out and sat down near

me. "What is your emergency, young man?"

"I need a better school. I don't want to be a butcher. The letter said it's too late, but in another year I'll be even older. I lost a whole year learning English. It takes a lot of years to be a doctor or a lawyer. I need a good school and I need to do it this fall. I want to work smart like my priest said."

All this explanation seemed to pour out of me. He just sat and took it in, rubbing his chin thoughtfully. "Can you pass the English test?"

"Maybe. Can you pass an Italian test?"

He laughed. "Probably not, but I have a master's degree in Latin. What kind of grades do you have in eighth grade?"

"All A's but B in English. I got *lodevole* in everything at *scuola media*. In Italy we only had to give the teacher pasta. Some people had to give silver to get *lodevole*."

"A remarkable grading system, I think. We don't do that here. No pasta. No silver. Just learn the material. I have a copy of the test in my office. Do you want to try it?"

My stomach was shaking but I said yes. I sat at a table near the secretary and worked away at the test. A couple of times I had to ask her about a word, and the priest said she could tell me. One part was really bad, matching up sets of words but the math was not so hard. I like math because it's either right or wrong and you don't have to explain. Finally I came to the end and handed it in. I wanted to beg the priest to let me in, but I had too much pride.

"I'll send you a letter," he said. "Ask the

principal at your school to send me a copy of your grades. Where did you go to grade school?"

"Santa Maria Addolorata."

"All the way over there? Are you going to be able to ride two buses every day and be on time?"

"I'll do it if I have to. Or I can walk. I used to walk to the harbor for fish. I'm a good walker, once my leg gets better."

As I got off the bus near home, Dom walked over. "Can you help me tonight, Peppino? Cookie has another job."

"You're still doing that, Dom? I thought you had a sponsor and a school. I thought you were going to learn how to fix cars."

"I just do it on the side, Peppino. Get a little money in my pocket. You know how it is."

"I can't do it, Dom. I have my own plans for my life."

"You're just afraid. I always knew you were a coward. You don't have what it takes to be a success."

"Big or not, it's my life, Dom. I'm going home. I have to get ready to work tomorrow." I turned away and started walking. Dom just stood there, staring at me, watching me go. That was it for me. We had a lot of fun when we were kids, but this was real life, and I was moving on. There's no gold on the streets here. I found that out. But I could get it. I just had to work for it.

# Author's Note

When Peppino and his mom arrived in America after the war, they found a world much different from their little town in Italy. Everything moved at a different pace and they were now living in a city of over 4 million (as of 1950) instead of about 1000. The neighborhood in the story attracted Italians as a majority, but there were people of many other nationalities as well.

Members of the underworld had many connections to politicians and law enforcement, enabling them to wield power in their areas. Not all of them were Italian, though many were. And just as now, organized criminal groups attracted young men by flashing a lot of cash and appearing successful. In the neighborhood around Grand Avenue and May, where the story is set, gangsters were a normal part of the landscape. Everyone knew them, and stayed out of their way.

The only real person named is Dan Brindisi, whose efforts to prevent delinquency and gangs earned him the honor of a street in Chicago named for him. Stories about mob influence in Chicago in the '50's can be found in histories and old newspapers of the era. The dialogs and events, though, are imaginary and people named are imagined for the sake of the story.

At that time many people coming to America to work entered illegally, usually coming off ships at New York. They were recruited and smuggled in by people known as *padroni* who extracted part of their wages as payback. Then, as now, the government arrested them when they were found, and sent them back home. Legal immigrants had to wait their turn. Peppino was able to bring his mother easily because his father had gained his citizenship years before. Families separated by the war were given early preference, but needed a sponsor who could guarantee their support.

In those days kids were expected to work to help their families and there were many odd jobs available. There were few safety restrictions on what young people could do. Most thought that an occasional accident was just a fact of life. Today no one would hire 14 year olds to dilute concentrated bleach and sell it in glass bottles. Nor would they be allowed to cut and sell meat, or babysit groups of children. Most transactions were cash, and only the few very richest paid income tax. Pay was low, but people managed to stretch their paycheck by bargaining, doing their own house and clothing repairs, and saving up for what they wanted.

# About the Author

Ann Rubino is the author of *Peppino, Good As Bread* (the prequel to *Peppino and the Streets of Gold*); *Le Forestiere* in the anthology, *Italian Women in Chicago*; and *Emmet's Storm*, an intermediate-grade novel about a boy genius at the turn of the century. As a child Ann Rubino read every book she could get her hands on, her favorites being the little orange biographies her mother gave her every Christmas. That began her lifelong love of learning. She gathered it first for herself, then to share with her children, and later to share with her students and other teachers. During those years she realized that many modern children are drawn to adventure, but often of a very fictional sort. It is monsters over inventors, superheroes over real ones. She wants to change that.

While Ann was teaching professionally, she won the OHAUS Award for innovations in science teaching; took part in the creation of the New Generation Science Standards; sat on the review board of *Science & Children* magazine; and worked as a consultant for the Museum of Science & Industry, Chicago. She holds her MT(ASCP), B.A.Ed., and M.S. Ed. and an Endorsement in Gifted Education. Her last teaching assignment was as adjunct at Lewis University, training future teachers in methods of science teaching. Once retired, she reviewed many children's books for the Recommends division of *Science & Children* and continued her work on the review board.

CPSIA information can be obtained at www.ICGtesting.com
Printed in the USA
LVOW11s1303120916

504204LV00016B/37/P

9 781942 247074